JULIA MURRAY

WED FOR
A WAGER

Complete and Unabridged

LINFORD
Leicester

First published in Great Britain in 1977 by
Robert Hale Limited
London

First Linford Edition
published 1998
by arrangement with
Roibert Hale Limited
London

British Library CIP Data

Murray, Julia
    Wed for a wager.—Large print ed.—
Linford romance library
1. Love stories
2. Large type books
I. Title
823.9'14 [F]

ISBN 0–7089–5253–4

Published by
F. A. Thorpe (Publishing) Ltd.
Anstey, Leicestershire

Set by Words & Graphics Ltd.
Anstey, Leicestershire
Printed and bound in Great Britain by
T. J. International Ltd., Padstow, Cornwall

This book is printed on acid-free paper

WED FOR A WAGER

When the wild Marquis of Veryan, the heir to a dukedom, is commanded by the Duke to take a wife or be cut off, he is certain all pleasure is at an end. But his mistress, Lady Elizabeth Sherreden, suggests a marriage with her sister-in-law. At first reluctant, Lord Veryan accepts a bet from his old adversary, Mr Waterhouse, to be married within the week. He proposes to Katharine Sherreden, and is accepted. All seems well, but Mr. Waterhouse is already plotting his revenge . . .

Books by Julia Murray
in the Linford Romance Library:

MASTER OF HERRINGHAM

1

THE door opened. His Grace, the Duke of Clayre, seated in a deep, winged chair at a distance from the fire, raised his head, and regarded the butler from beneath his shaggy white brows.

"So, John, he has come."

"Yes, your Grace." The man approached and set the port and a glass on the small table beside the Duke. "I have put him in Lord Peter's room, your Grace. I hope you find that appropriate."

The brilliant blue eyes twinkled. "His father's room, eh? Well enough, well enough. Give him a sense of occasion, not that one can ever be without it in this barrack of a place."

'This barrack of a place' was in fact Castle Clayre, situated in Northumberland, close to the Cumberland and

Scottish borders. It was an ancient fortress, built as protection against the marauding Scots, and for three months of the year almost invariably inaccessible except by foot. Isolated as it was, it suited his Grace very well since it encouraged none of his many relations to pay him visits when the duns were running close.

The Duke watched critically as his man poured the ruby liquid into the glass, grunted, and raised it to his lips. "Shan't see him tonight, John," he said presently, setting the glass down. "Won't do him any harm to be kept kicking his heels for a while. And John, when he asks for me in the morning, tell him I've gone for my walk. No sense in letting him think he's been summoned here to see me into my coffin."

"Very good, your Grace. And at what time do you wish to take your walk?"

"Same time, John, same time." The old man chuckled. "Angry, is he? Ha! Just as well!" he considered his grandson a moment longer, and then said: "Tell me, John, how's he looking?"

"As far as I could judge, your Grace, very healthy."

"No sign of any junketing, then?"

"I wouldn't like to say that, exactly, your Grace."

"Ha! So Edward was right, eh?" The butler preserved a discreet silence. "Very well, very well, don't stand there poker-faced! Get about your business!" John bowed, and withdrew.

A few minutes later the Marquis of Veryan, sitting alone in a vast and chilly drawing room, was nettled to discover that his grandfather had apparently no intention of joining him for dinner. It had taken him three days to get there, and the road up from the village had been rough enough to make him sincerely hope it had all been worth his while. The castle was enormous and very crafty, and he had been hoping to get the interview over as soon as possible that he might return to London on the morrow. Now it seemed as though it was not to be. His grandfather might be an ancient and eccentric old man, but he had summoned Lord Veryan, who felt it reasonable that some attention might now be given him.

He was not without hope, however. The summons had come at a time when he was considering rusticating for a while, and although a journey to the far North of England was not precisely what he wished for, he was not yet without expectations of it turning out well. The suspicion that his Grace was at last about to join his ancestors could not but occur to him. A little quick arithmetic satisfied him that the old man must be seventy at the very least, and although he had little desire to step into the old man's shoes, they would bring with them a great many advantages he could ill do without.

The excellent but slightly cold dinner did much to restore his spirits, and he began to reflect that it might not be so very bad to be a duke after all. Not that he would inhabit Castle Clayre, of course. Not only was it over two hundred miles from all his interests, but it was a dashed unpleasant place, full of dark corners, secret passages, and history.

At ten o'clock Lord Veryan sighed, and made his way from the dining room to his father's chamber. This move had irritated him; he would much rather have been allocated the room he had inhabited as a boy, which was at least made pleasant by memories. The dark and lofty apartment in which he now found himself had always had a gloomy aspect, and was made so by the knowledge of to whom it had belonged. Lord Veryan discovered his valet in the act of laying out his night-shirt, and of a sudden his situation amused him. He began to appreciate his grandfather's intentions, and it occurred to him that he would, in fact, be very sorry to learn of the old gentleman's demise, since he had always liked him a great deal better than any other of his relations. He chuckled softly, and submitted patiently to Peeble's administrations. Dashed if it would not be good to see the old man again, he thought, as his man carefully arranged the mountain of covers beneath his chin. He settled back comfortably on the pile of pillows with the intention of reviewing his rather embarrassing situation in town, but he was more tired than he had thought, and the effort of addition seen deprived him of consciousness.

He awoke the next morning considerably refreshed, and not a little surprised at how well he had slept. The light that penetrated through the narrow window assured him of a pleasant day, and he was up and peering out with a rapidity which, had he considered it, would greatly have surprised him. He was a young man, barely twenty-four, tall and loose-limbed, with unruly brown hair that tended to fall into his eyes. These were large and blue, and held a look of innocence that was belied by some slight lines of dissipation that already marred his youthful countenance. He was, in fact, a wild young man, and had at one time been an object of despair for his father. This gentleman, however, had been dead five years, and Lord Veryan, coming into a certain amount of independence at the age of nineteen, had wasted no time in sampling the delights of an unshackled existence. The Duke, his guardian, had sent him to Oxford, for he was not unintelligent, but he had remained there barely a term before he had transgressed so far as to be sent down. Whereupon his grandfather, apart from adjuring a helpful nephew to 'keep an eye on the brat', had washed his hands of him. The nephew, a portly gentleman of forty-five, had done more than either the grandfather or grandson had envisaged. He adopted some of a parent's duties, lecturing and scolding the young man, and paying periodic visits to the Duke in order to report on the heir's erratic progress. Lord Veryan regarded him with disgust, and his Grace, by whom Sir Edward's secret hopes had long been known, with contempt.

The Marquis, anxious to impress a man he had not seen for more than two years, dressed with more than usual care that morning, selecting his second best fob, and ruining five neckcloths before he achieved a result that satisfied him. He felt quite cheerful as he sauntered down to the breakfast room, but he was there greeted by the intelligence that his Grace had gone for a walk and would not be back for an hour. This news quite killed the view that he had been summoned to a death-bed interview, but, instead of feeling relief, his lordship experienced a strong sensation of pique. He had half a mind to go for a walk too in the hope that he might encounter his Grace, but the recollection that these walks were almost invariably long, and never in the same direction two days together, quite quashed this idea. He attempted to banish his ill-humour, and, having satisfied his appetite, went out to review his acquaintance with the immediate grounds.

It was November, and not warm, but the sun was bright, and the castle appeared to advantage. It was an enormous building, of Norman beginnings, but with much added to the original square keep. The latest addition had been made in the sixteenth century, and was a quadrant in Tudor style, which, though fine, gave the castle a motley look. Lord Veryan passed the hour more pleasurably than he had expected. He discovered, quite by chance, an old arrow of his, stuck deep into the bark of an ancient oak, half covered with foliage. In remembering the day on which it had been fired, and the hours he had spent looking for it, the time passed rapidly, and it was not long before the clock in the bell tower was striking noon. He returned at once to the house, the arrow still in his hand, and on entering the castle was greeted by John, who informed him that his Grace would be happy to see him in his private sitting-room. His lordship was conscious of momentary nervousness as he followed the butler up the familiar passages, and with a rueful smile remembered the occasions he had been summoned to attend the Duke in his apartment, almost invariably for some misdemeanour. The recollection made him grin, and consequently it was an extraordinarily youthful-looking gentleman who was bowed into the spacious and comfortable apartment. The room being in the newer part of the building, the window by which his Grace was standing was large and light, and his grandson's first impression was that he looked amazingly healthy. Then the Duke turned round, and caught the last glimpse of the grin as it faded from his grandson's face.

"Humph," he said, walking easily into the centre of the room. He was very straight, and had no recourse to a stick. "So you're here. Took long enough about it, didn't you?"

Lord Veryan, well-acquainted with his Grace's brusque manner, merely grinned anew, and said he had come as soon as the letter was received.

"Damned post," muttered his Grace, catching his glass and raising it to his eye. Through it he calmly scrutinized his grandson.

"Humph", he said, critically remarking the young man's attire. "Seems to me you're becoming a dashed dandy!"

The tone was severe, but the Marquis merely grinned. He took some efforts with his appearance, and his tail-coat of dark blue superfine and biscuit-coloured pantaloons were, in fact, all the crack. In deference to his grandfather he had effected an arrangement for his cravat less elaborate than usual, but his shirt-points were heavily starched and reached almost to his ears.

"I don't know what you young men are coming to," declared his Grace, letting fall his glass and moving to a chair. "In my day no gentleman would be seen abroad without his wig, and as for those newfangled things!" He jerked his thumb at the young man's pantaloons, and lowered himself into a chair. "I'm only thankful that the day will never come when you see such things at Court!" He made an impatient gesture to his grandson, who correctly interpreted it as an indication to be seated, taking care all the while not to crease his tails or render his pantaloons disgraceful with a wrinkle. The old man watched his manoeuvres from beneath his shaggy brows, and barely repressed a snort. "I suppose you thought to find me on my death-bed, eh?"

Since this had been precisely Lord Veryan's expectation he reddened as he disclaimed, at which the old man chuckled.

"Then you're a fool," he remarked frankly. "Dashed long-lived family, the Carradales. My father died at seventy-five. Would have lived longer but for some foolishness. Insisted on taking a walk in the snow. Caught his death. All long-lived, as would your father have been, if he hadn't been so stupid as to fall down the stairs and break his neck! Ha!" His Grace chuckled again, and regarded his grandson keenly from beneath his heavy white eyebrows. "Well, now, so you obeyed my summons, eh? Some mighty pretty things I've been hearing about you, and no mistake!"

Lord Veryan grinned unperturbed. "Do I gather Edward has been to see you, sir?"

His Grace smiled reluctantly. "Damned impertinent! Thought I'd like to know, he said! Ha! Sent him away with a flea in his ear and no mistake! However, that ain't what I want to talk to you about. Don't like Edward, never have, but he's a lot more up to snuff than you, sir! Not one to stand with tittle-tattle, boy, but when it comes to affairs with married women, well, that's something too near a scandal for me!"

Lord Veryan reddened uncomfortably.

"There, now, lad, don't get flushed up about it. Dashed hard, a lad of your age, accepting such responsibilities. But they're yours, and have been for five years or more. You've had long enough to get used to it by now. What I want to know is, when are you going to settle?"

Lord Veryan raised his brows.

"Settled, lad!" repeated his Grace. "Leg-shackled, married!"

Lord Veryan stared, and then smiled. "Well, sir, to tell truth, I haven't thought about it. It's not as though I'm old, after all, and as you say, there's no chance of my acceding for ten years or more."

His Grace's blue eyes regarding the young man very hard. "Now see here, sir, I'm not jesting! I know very well what Edward wants, but he's not one for farradiddles. It won't do, sir, for you to be gallivanting in this way. You owe it to your name to avoid scandal. So this is what I've decided to do. I can't stop you acceding, and I can't stop Castle Clayre being yours one day. However, there's Stannisburn and Cheard which are my own property. It pains me to say this, lad, but those houses, plus what is untied in the Funds, will go to Edward if you don't mend your ways. The word is you're in deep water. Well I'm not surprised, the way you've been burning blunt, and you'll find soon enough that without funds Clayre is impossible to maintain. You need Cheard, and Stannisburn even more, if you are to make good. I dislike Edward, but he's sensible, and he won't waste my money as you would. But then I've no mind to cut you out. So here's your choice. Take a wife, boy. Settle down, and I'll make you a present of Stannisburn on your wedding day. It's a fine house, your father liked it, and it'll give you a good income. I don't mind who she is, as long as the name is good. Do this, Christopher, and I'll settle twenty-thousand on you, and another twenty on your heir." He stopped, and regarded the young man keenly.

Lord Veryan rose without a word and crossed to the window. He was rather pale, but although greatly confused, gave no other sign of inner turmoil. He disliked the ultimatum, yet in spite of all could not deny his grandfather's right to dispose of his property as he wished, and also to demand a modicum of decorum from his heir. It cost him much to admit this, but he was not given to self-deceit, and he knew he had been playing a dangerous game.

The Duke, meanwhile, sat silent. He had a certain reluctant respect for his grandson, and was pleased that the young man had not succumbed to the violent rage he had expected. What was more he had been wild in his own youth, and knew well that by imposing such an ultimatum he was exposing himself to the young man's hatred. He had not forgotten his own part in his heir's upbringing, and had realized that much blame lay at his door for not taking his grandson earlier in hand.

After a while Lord Veryan turned from the window and approached the old man again. He was pale, but calm, and man the Duke a stiff bow. "Very well, sir, I accede to your demands. May I know how long I am to have?"

His Grace regarded the young man with something like affection. "Until the end of the season."

"I am grateful. I shall endeavour to do as you ask."

"Thank you. Ring the bell for John. Sit down, and drink with me. There's no need to rush, you know, just because we're agreed. John, claret, if you please."

Lord Veryan accepted the glass thoughtfully, and sat staring into the red liquid for several minutes. His Grace did not disturb him, but by motioning to his butler was provided with a stout box and the appropriate key. A few minutes later the Marquis was startled by having a fat roll of bills tossed in front of him. He stared at his grandfather, thoughtfully fingering the roll. "I am grateful, but perhaps I ought to know what you expect from me in return."

"Devil take you, boy! In deep water, ain't you? Pay your bills."

"As I say, sir, I am grateful, but I'd as lief not accept it until I have acceded to your demands."

"On your high horse now, are you. See here, lad, that's something different, from me to my grandson, do you understand?"

The young man looked up then, and smiled slightly. "Thank you, sir, I'm grateful." He drained his glass, and stood up. "If you will pardon me, I think I will start. It's barely one; I shall get twenty miles or so today."

"Ha! Come to see your grandfather, do you, and leave as soon as you can!"

He smiled. "I have a lot to do, sir, and I'd as lief begin before I think too much! Shall you be at Cheard?"

"Ay, in a few days. John's got a touch of gout, though he don't admit to it, and that fool who calls himself my doctor says I'm not what I used to be. So we'll try the waters at Bath. Bring her la'ship to visit, if you will."

Lord Veryan grinned. "I will, sir, but you're as strong as an ox, as well you know! But come if you wish. I shan't disappoint you."

"No, lad, I know you won't."

2

THE Marquis of Veryan returned to London in a mood of deep depression. This was not even alleviated by the thought that, with the money in his pocket and the small fortune that would soon be his, there was no need for him to dispose of his elegant travelling carriage or the team that drew it, and that his curricle, the matched bays, and several riding horses were equally safe. Although despondent, he was not bitter; in fact, the more he thought about it, the more surprised he became that he had not been brought to heel earlier. He had known very well that Sir Edward Carradale reported his every move to his grandfather, and could even admit now that the fact that his cousin's eye had been upon him had encouraged him in even greater excesses. When he thought of Elizabeth, however, he knew some regrets.

The Lady Elizabeth Sherreden had been the lady who had finally provoked his grandfather's wrath. She was a beautiful little piece with corn-gold hair and enormous, melting blue eyes. She had certainly captivated his lordship on her first appearance, and his attraction for her had by no means been lessened by her marriage. Sir Robert was an indolent husband, who, following his own pursuits, was content to let his wife follow hers, provided she was always discreet. There was little love in the case. Miss Elizabeth Slaidburn had been a considerable heiress, Sir Robert Sherreden a baronet. Therein lay the attraction. Miss Slaidburn had had hopes of ensnaring the Marquis himself, but this gentleman, although delighting in flirtation, had shied clear of marriage at an early age. And it had proved an admirable arrangement. Lady Elizabeth, instead of being lost to him on her marriage, had in reality been more available than ever, and he had never regretted not marrying her. Until now, that is. If only he had taken the little lady when she had shown herself so willing his Grace would have been happy, and he would, moreover, have come into a very neat sum from his wife. And now he had it all to do.

It never occurred to him to flout the Duke. He was a man of his word, and Lord Veryan knew that however much it cost him the Duke would leave everything he could to Sir Edward if he did not comply. And this, apart from the value of the property, would pain Lord Veryan. Stannisburn, in Hampshire, had been his home for many years. His father had loved it, and Lord Veryan himself was in the habit of spending his summer months there. To lose this, and to Sir Edward, would be bitter indeed. He had a little property of his own, a small hunting box in Leicestershire, but it was a recent acquisition, and brought in none of the revenues Lord Veryan so desperately needed.

On his second day of travelling Lord Veryan forced his mind to review the ladies of his acquaintance. It was a bleak past-time. Swaying with the coach he carelessly jotted down the names of some half dozen young ladies, and then, one by one, crossed them all out. One was too old, another crooked teeth, a third a horribly affected laugh. Eventually he threw the tablet away in disgust. That was no way to choose a wife. He had several months — time enough to become acquainted with a presentable female.

He reached London early the following evening. His depression had resolved itself into a mood of resignation, but he still felt low enough to dine in his lodgings on what his landlady had managed to produce at very short notice. He had brooded for some time over his port before, having drained his third glass, he sat up very straight, and made a rapid decision.

Pushing his chair back hastily he quitted the room. A half hour saw him nattily attired in the dark coat and satin knee-breeches indispensable for an evening's entertainment and striding up Arlington Street towards Piccadilly. Dodging the carriages and sedan chairs he was in Berkeley Street in a moment and heading purposefully for the residence of Lady Jefford. So occupied had he been with his problems that he had forgotten Lady Jefford and the fact that he had been engaged for her evening party for several weeks. It did not promise to be a very splendid affair. Most of the society families were out of town, but he had reason to believe that Sir Robert Sherreden was not, and that he and his lovely wife would be in Berkeley Street that very evening.

He was not the last to arrive, but it was a pre-season party and guests were usually expected earlier than at the height of London's festivities, when several balls and parties might be attended in one evening. As he mounted the broad, sweeping stairway to the first floor sounds of merriment that accorded so ill with his present mood floated down to him, and he knew a momentary impulse to turn back. He did not, however, and pursued his leisurely way upstairs.

Lady Jefford was pleased to see him. The news that he was out of town had reached her earlier, and she was agreeably flattered that he had decided to come. In spite of his slightly careless and rakish air he was a general favourite, possessed of a tolerable figure, and a smile that charmed the ladies. It was not in evidence tonight, however. Lady Jefford, her bosom impressively swathed in purple satin, was a large, indolent female, not usually alive to the moods of others, but Lord Veryan this evening wore such a tired, melancholy air that even she was aware of it. Beckoning to a servant she thoughtfully provided him with a glass of champagne, and proceeded to engage him in conversation.

Across the room a diminutive little lady, exquisitely attired in floating blue gauze with an under-dress that clung so tightly to her form that it could only have been damped, watched him somewhat speculatively. Although she had not expected to see him she had nevertheless marked his entrance, and for some minutes had been inattentive to the modish young gentleman at her elbow. The Marquis's haggard appearance and tired air were not lost on her, and she took her first opportunity of smiling brilliantly up at her cavalier and sending him off for champagne. Then she crossed the room with small, brisk steps, and stationed herself before Lord Veryan and her hostess.

The precise nature of the relationship between Lady Sherreden and Lord Veryan was not known, but it was generally acknowledged that each was rather better acquainted with the other than was precisely necessary. Lady

Jefford, however, after one glance at Lord Veryan's face, came rapidly to the conclusion that she was definitely *de trop*, and hastily moved away. It was no business of hers what these young people got up to, but she did wish, just sometimes, that these little intrigues were not *quite* so fashionable.

A brief examination of his lordship's face assured Lady Sherreden that her judgement had not been at fault. The visit to Northumberland had brought something quite other than he had expected before he left.

"Elizabeth, I must talk to you."

"Yes, my dear, I know, but not here."

"Where, then? I must speak to you tonight."

Another glance at him assured her that this was so. After thinking rapidly for a moment she turned her face up to him and said quickly: "There is a balcony. I will take some air. Come to me in a moment."

In spite of his state Lord Veryan

laughed. "My little love, you will freeze to death on the balcony in that dress!"

"I daresay I shall, but it is of no consequence. Only do not leave me there too long." She looked up at him affectionately and then hurried across the room towards a window in the far corner. Her progress was somewhat hampered by the return of her gallant with champagne, but she disposed of him somehow and in a moment had slipped unobtrusively behind the heavy brocade curtains. A minute or two later and Lord Veryan crossed the room himself in a leisurely way, exchanging words with several people as he went, seemingly in no hurry. He stood for a moment leaning against the wall, and then, when he thought no one was watching, slipped behind the curtain and out of sight. As he had expected he found Lady Sherreden shivering violently.

"Oh, my lord!" she exclaimed as soon as she saw him, "thank heaven you are come! I thought I should die of cold if I stayed a moment longer!"

Lord Veryan smiled, and, taking her shawl, wrapped it more expeditiously about her white shoulders. Then he put his arm round her and drew her close. "It is finished, Elizabeth, between us. I must not see you again."

Lady Sherreden, who had been lying comfortably within his arms, stiffened suddenly and looked up at him, her alarm apparent even in the half-light. "No, no, and *no!* Oh, Christopher, what do you mean?"

Lord Veryan sighed. He had known it would not be easy, and Lady Sherreden had apparently no intention of sparing him. "My cousin Carradale has observed us. He has told my grandfather everything. I must give you up, Elizabeth, or he will cut me off."

"That horrid Sir Edward! Well, I knew he had been watching us, but I never realized he could be so mean as to report on us. But tell me, how can the Duke cut you off? Are you not his legal heir?"

"Yes, my love, but I'm entitled only to Clayre, and some small amount in the Funds. Everything else, Stannisburn, Cheard, the town house, will go to Edward unless I leave you. And I must say it, I cannot let that happen."

"But Christopher, am I to be sacrificed merely for money? No, you could not be so heartless!"

"My love, you do not understand what it means to be without money! You have always had so much! What my mother left me was wasted long ago, and my father, since he never acceded, left me barely a living! I must do as he asks!"

Lady Sherreden was silent. She still lay against him, but her body was rigid within his arms, her face turned away. After a little while, however, she turned to him again, her expression strained and anxious. "Christopher, must it be over completely? We have been indiscreet, but I could be more careful, my darling, indeed I could! Only do not say I must never see you again!"

Lord Veryan pulled a long yellow curl affectionately. "If that were all! My love, I have not been completely honest with you. The Duke orders me to marry. That is the condition."

For a moment Lady Sherreden stared at him uncomprehendingly, and then she pulled herself away, and stood with her back to him, her head bowed, shivering. Lord Veryan did not move. He had not believed her to care so much for him, and it was a shock to discover, now, that she apparently cared deeply.

After a while the golden head was raised and Lady Sherreden moved to the wrought iron barrier to look out over the garden. Running her finger absently along the painted metal she seemed deep in contemplation, which was confirmed a few minutes later when she swung round suddenly, her face alive and radiant.

"Oh, my Christopher!" she exclaimed, running joyfully back to him. "I have it, the perfect solution! What a fool

I was not to think of it earlier! You must marry Katty!"

Lord Veryan stared at her uncomprehendingly.

"Katty," she repeated impatiently. "Robert's sister!"

Enlightenment dawned, and a look of amazement crossed his face. "Miss Sherreden?" he ejaculated. "Lizzy, are you run mad? I daresay she is a very good sort of girl, but — Elizabeth have you thought what it would mean?"

"Yes, yes!" she cried joyfully. "We would be meeting forever! It would be perfect! No one could say anything about our being in each other's company, for you would be my brother, and what could be more unexceptional than that?"

"Dash it, Lizzy, even supposing — no, it's preposterous!"

"Why? Why is it preposterous? Are you thinking that she hasn't any money? Because if you are, that's ridiculous, since you would have plenty yourself!"

"Even so, why should she accept

me? Surely she knows the relationship between us?"

Lady Sherreden shrugged. "I daresay she might, but I don't see that it matters. As for accepting you, I know she will. She's been unhappy with us, you know. Robert always resented her, and although he always had to keep her, he's never done more than he needed." She reflected a moment. "I haven't been very nice to her either, but then it's so horrid having poor relations about all the time, especially other people's. I think she would accept anybody, just to get away from us! And then you'd be able to give her everything she wants, you know. Oh, it's perfect, Christopher, don't you see?"

He looked down at her a moment. "No," he said shortly, "I don't."

"Well," she exclaimed angrily, "I think you are very mean, indeed. I do! I show you how everything can be perfectly alright again and you throw it back in that odious way! Do you think so little of me?"

Lord Veryan sighed. He was fond of Lady Sherreden, but there were two reasons why he found her proposal objectionable. Since he had to marry, it was not in his mind to take a penniless young woman glad of any home she could get. If he must have a wife she might as well be rich. Secondly, wild and irresponsible he might be, but he did not wish to start his married life by taking a girl who must know all about his less savoury activities, and who, moreover, would be obliged to turn a blind eye to their continuance. He did not think it would augur well for their happiness. He had decided, in fact, to finish with Lady Sherreden, and marriage with her husband's young half-sister was not part of his plan.

He became aware of her looking anxiously up at him, and realized that a reply was necessary. He knew he ought to tell her now, but his affection, though not deep, was sincere, and would not permit him to be so blunt. He temporized, therefore, and finally persuaded her back to the drawing room. It was his intention to mingle with the other guests from then on, but he felt constrained, before parting with Elizabeth, to adjure her to say nothing to anyone. It occurred to him that she might put the suggestion to Miss Sherreden herself.

Lord Veryan was a little perturbed. He had been sure that her affection was no deeper than his own, that she, like him, had been anxious only for a little illicit amusement and fun. Now it appeared as though it were not so. Her display seemed to indicate a deeper affection than he had any idea of, and it confirmed him in his resolve to part from her completely. It grieved him to pain her, but he knew very well that anything else would be a disaster.

In so judging Lady Sherreden's motives, however, Lord Veryan was in error. She was fond of him — she had found him attractive from the start, and it amused her to carry on a flagrant affair in front of her husband. The idea, however, that he should leave her, and with so small a struggle, was damaging to her pride, and she did not mean to let it happen.

The plan of his marrying Katharine had seemed perfect from the first. She had little affection for her sister-in-law, and disliked her continual, dampening presence in the house. She believed her to be unaware of the true nature of her affair with the Marquis, and the idea of carrying off Katharine's husband's affections from beneath her nose was vastly appealing. She had no doubt of her power with him, and believed she would succeed in the end. To be sure, his opposition had daunted her a little; she had, in fact, been quite put out, but it had taken her a very few minutes to realize that he was still distressed, and that she had merely been too hasty. Although this cheered her, she did not, when Lord Veryan glanced at her later, let him know it. It would never do to let him think she could be happy; she was shrewd enough to know that a sorrowful, wilting countenance would be far more likely to carry the point. She saw him concerned, and was satisfied.

3

LORD VERYAN slept late the next morning. He had not remained over-long in Berkeley Street, but his thoughts had kept him awake far into the small hours. When he finally opened his eyes it was to feel far from refreshed. In fact, he seemed hardly to have slept at all.

The night had brought him no counsel, and this morning his problems weighed as heavily as they had ever done. Tossing off the bed-clothes he padded to the window and peered out on a grey cheerless day. He sighed. No riding, then. Much though he wished to, he did not feel that staying within would do him any good. He decided, therefore, to take a leisurely stroll round to Boodle's and seek the advice of his friends. Now that he was resolved to marry he had decided not to put off the evil hour. Delay would only result in undesirable reflection. A visit to his club, therefore, seemed called for. One of his cronies would certainly know of a suitable, acceptable female.

He found them in a mood of depressing joviality. A little group had congregated about the wide fireplace in one of the drawing rooms, and Lord Veryan, although he sauntered across the room towards them, nevertheless puckered his brow at the sight of one Mr George Waterhouse. A slight animosity existed between the two. It was well concealed, and, since they shared a great many friends, each managed to hide their feelings from the others in their set. It was doubtful whether any knew of it, confined as it was to one or two extravagant and daring bets, and the occasional challenge to a horse, or curricle race. Nevertheless Mr Waterhouse disliked the Marquis and knew very well that his feelings were reciprocated. He was a tall, well-looking gentleman with dark, almost black hair, and a certain supercilious curl to his thin lips. His quiet flair in dress always managed to excite his lordship's reluctant envy. Mr Waterhouse knew it, and it amused him. As he approached the Marquis ran an eye up Mr. Waterhouse's immaculate person, and was forced to admit that, whatever the fellow might be like, he had a way of dressing himself that Lord Veryan had never quite mastered. Nothing could have been more perfect than the set of Mr Waterhouse's olive tail-coat across shoulders that had no need of padding, and the pale pantaloons clung enviably to a pair of finely shaped legs. A single fob dangling at his waist and a fine diamond pin in the folds of his cravat were the only jewellery he effected, but the Marquis had to admit that the result was elegant. Mr Waterhouse raised his quizzing glass now, and watched Lord Veryan's progress across the room. Another of the group, a tall, sandy-haired gentleman with a Belcher hankerchief carelessly knotted about his throat, also spotted him.

"Good God!" he exclaimed, staring at him out of wide-apart blue eyes. "If it ain't Ver! What you looking so dashed dull for? Old man still alive?"

"As strong as a horse," corroborated Lord Veryan gloomily, joining Mr Malling by the fire.

"Thought so," remarked a youthful-looking gentleman sapiently. "Never die when you want 'em to. Wait till the dibs are in tune again, then they pop off, calm as you please. Should have known it, Ver, before you went. Told you."

"Dash it, Barton, how could you know?" demanded his lordship irritably. "He's seventy-five at the very least, and Clayre's a cursed draughty place, too."

"Kill you, draughts," remarked a slight young gentleman nattily attired in a coat of dark-blue superfine cloth with pearl buttons who had been thoughtfully sucking one corner of his handkerchief. "Killed an aunt of mine, once, a draught. No point in it, though. Left it all to some plaguey son."

"You'll know next time, anyway," said Mr. Barton, nodding. "Get the dibs in tune, and he'll pop off right enough. Be a duke then," he added, as an afterthought. Mr Malling nodded, and they lapsed into silence.

"You at Lady Jeff's last night?" asked Mr Malling after a moment. "Daresay you know about it, then."

Lord Veryan, who had nodded, rolled his eyes heavenwards and demanded testily: "Know about what, Freddie, for the lord's sake?"

"The Winslow necklace. Stolen. Thought you'd know."

"No, I don't, and I shan't either, by the looks of it!"

"Alright, Ver, alright!" said Mr Malling soothingly. "Though how you came to be there and know nothing I can't imagine. Perhaps you'd already left," he suggested, after a moment.

"I daresay that's it," Lord Veryan agreed, impatiently, "but I wish you'd tell me what happened."

"Well, it seems Lady Jeff was wearing the thing, diamonds and rubies, all night. Then someone sent a message by one of the lackeys that he wanted to see her on the balcony, and when she got there he just pulled them off her. Terrible fuss. Called in the Watch, but no sign of the fellow."

"Good Gad!" exclaimed the Marquis, astonished. "You say he just took them? Who was it?"

"Dash it, Ver, do you think if they knew that they'd have the Runners out? Stupid lackey can't remember. It was dark on the balcony, so Lady Jeff didn't see. Just took them, and jumped down into the garden. Quite simple, really."

"Dashed simple," agreed the Marquis, thoughtfully. "It must have happened after I left. Pity. I could have done with cheering up. Funny thing is, I was on that balcony myself last night. Ah, well."

"Rum business," said Mr Malling. "Surprised you don't know. Had it

43

from Stowing, who was there, saw it all. Not the theft, of course, but the fuss. Lady Jeff had a fit of the vapours."

"Good God!" exclaimed the Marquis disgustedly. "If that's so I'm glad I wasn't there! Vapours! Nothing worse!"

Mr Malling nodded, and they lapsed into silence once more.

"Heard about Wisley?" demanded Mr Barton after a moment. "Dashed rum thing."

"Don't be an idiot, Bart," said Mr Malling. "Ver's only been gone two days. Of course he knows."

"No he ain't," protested Mr. Barton, mildly indignant. "Left town on Thursday. More than a week. Doesn't know about Wisley."

"Never mind when I left. What's he done? Shot himself at last?"

"Devil a bit," answered Mr Barton with a smile. "Getting married."

"Married?" echoed his lordship, stunned. "She's never accepted him?"

"She has," nodded the slight young

gentleman, entering the conversation again. "On Monday. Going to be announced."

"Good God!" exclaimed Lord Veryan, accepting this indisputable evidence. "If that don't beat all!"

"That's what I thought," nodded the sandy-haired Mr. Malling gloomily. "Don't know what got into the fellow. Or her, come to that. Sorry, Dex, I keep forgetting she's your cousin."

The slight young gentleman, finding himself thus addressed, jumped, and blushed. "So do I," he said simply.

"Dash it, Dexter," exclaimed Lord Veryan irritably. "Sometimes I think you've got a screw loose! How can you forget Anabel's your cousin?"

Lord Dexter shrugged. "I don't know. Seems easy enough, though."

"Got too many relations, Dex," said Mr Malling, discovering his snuff-box after a brief search. "Try some of my sort, Ver?"

Lord Veryan declined politely, and returned to the subject that was interesting him most. "Where's Wisley now? Gone out of town?"

"Devil a bit," responded Mr Malling, carefully inhaling a pinch of snuff. "He's all over town, telling 'em how happy he is. Wouldn't have thought it myself, but you never know with these baronets. I daresay they'll be happy enough."

"But what did he want to *marry* the girl for?" demanded Lord Veryan, his own situation uppermost in his mind.

"Dash it, Ver, what else could he do?" demanded Mr Malling, rolling an eye in Lord Veryan's direction. "Female of that sort, nothing else he could do."

Lord Dexter, who had been painstakingly following this conversation, inferred an insult to his cousin from this remark, and stepped forward angrily. His friends, understanding after a moment what he was at, were at some pains to calm him.

"What I can't understand," mused Lord Veryan, returning to what was, at that moment, an overriding concern, "is why Wisley thought he would be happier married."

Mr Malling pondered this. "Known her all her life," he offered at last.

"That don't mean a thing, Freddie," the Marquis pointed out with an air of logic. "They always change as soon as they're married. It's inevitable." He pondered this for a moment. "It seems to me, Freddie, that if you're going to be married at all it may as well be to someone you don't know. That way at least you get to know the real woman. They leave off all their airs after they're married."

Mr Malling looked at him. "You seem to have given it a deal of thought, Ver, I must say."

Lord Veryan shrugged. "All I say is, there's no reason to suppose Wisley will be happy just because he's known her a long time. In my opinion he's known her too long."

Mr Malling considered his friend from beneath his sandy brows. "What's

47

come over you, Ver? You were never wont to be so serious."

"I believe he's jealous," remarked Mr Waterhouse with a cool smile, entering the conversation for the first time. "He knows no one would accept him, whether she knew him or not!"

"Going to be a duke," pointed out Lord Dexter fairly. "Like to be duchesses, females do."

"Well, I must say, George, I think you have been a little unfair to poor Ver! Not to say he's much of a catch now, but as Dex says, he will be before long!"

"Dash it, Freddie, why shouldn't I get married?" demanded Lord Veryan, stung. "I dare swear I'm as good a catch as the next man!"

"So you say, dear fellow," chuckled Mr. Waterhouse, tauntingly. "Have to admit you're not very reliable, though."

"Not reliable!" exclaimed the Marquis, reddening rapidly. "Explain yourself, George!"

"Take it easy, dear fellow. I don't

mean anything at all!" Nevertheless his dark eyes twinkled with amusement.

"I daresay I could be married before you, at any rate," declared his lordship, keeping a hold on his temper with difficulty.

"Purely hypothetical, my dear Veryan, since there is no prospect of a decent woman taking you that I can see."

"Steady, George, what are you thinking of?" said Mr Malling, eyeing Lord Veryan somewhat apprehensively.

Lord Dexter removed his handkerchief from his mouth. "Let Ver prove it, then," he said.

All four gentlemen swung round. The young lord, startled to discover the amount of attention he had drawn to himself, blushed scarlet, and returned to his contemplation of the fireplace.

"By Jove!" exclaimed Mr Waterhouse, pleased. "If that don't beat all! How about it, Veryan? Get married, and prove me wrong!"

Mr Malling's jaw dropped. "Can't do that, old fellow," he protested. "A man don't have to get married, you know. Ver's only saying he could. Can't force it on him."

Lord Veryan, who had been fixing Mr Waterhouse with a strange look, laid his hand on Mr Malling's arm. "No, no, Freddie, I've a mind to take him up. Did you mean it, George?"

Mr. Waterhouse, although surprised, nodded decisively.

"Then I accept. Name your terms."

"Ver!" exclaimed Mr. Malling, horrified. "You can't do that! George has no right to demand it of you, have you, George?"

Mr Waterhouse, an amused smile on his face, said nothing.

"Name your terms, George," repeated Lord Veryan.

Mr Waterhouse, carefully flicking a speck of dust from his olive sleeve, eyed him coolly. "Well, it's not easy, Veryan, you know. I've a mind to take you up on the acquaintance part." He frowned in an effort of concentration. "Put up a hundred, my lord, be married within a week, and I'll give you odds of five to one."

Lord Veryan paled. Mr. Malling gasped.

"Those are my terms, my lord," said Mr. Waterhouse, characteristically calm.

Lord Veryan thought rapidly. Five hundred pounds would be very useful, but he was, for a moment, at a loss for a suitable female. A week would give him time to do little more than make the necessary arrangements, of which fact Mr. Waterhouse was clearly aware. He glanced up, and saw Mr. Waterhouse smiling. It annoyed him to refuse a wager, even this wager, but where could he find a suitable female?

That was when he remembered. She was by no means ideal, and would bring him into contact with Lady Sherreden that he did not want, but at that moment only Katharine Sherreden occurred to him. He made a quick decision.

"Very well, George, but not, if you please, the betting book. I should not like my wife to know I married her for a bet."

Mr. Malling choked.

"I'm agreeable, Veryan," said Mr. Waterhouse, holding his hand out obligingly. He glanced at his watch. "How convenient! It is nearly noon. A week today, then, Veryan. Time enough, I think."

Lord Veryan nodded, his brain working fast. He made a slight bow. "Will you excuse me, gentlemen, I have business to tend to." He left them then, and Mr. Malling, who had for some time been feeling weak at the knees, sat down in a hurry.

Lord Veryan strode quickly into St. James's Street and there stopped. His determination had carried him out of the drawing room and down the stairs, but now in the street the utter foolishness of his actions struck him. He began to realize that he was on the verge of what the evening before he had had no intention of doing, and had very nearly walked to Upper Grosvenor Street on the impulse. Now he started thinking hard. To back out would mean the loss of a hundred pounds, which he could ill-afford. A politely worded letter from his tailor had been delivered only that morning, and it would not do merely to order a new suit of clothes. But apart from the money his credit with his friends would suffer, and this he was loath to bear, particularly when the opposite party was one Mr. Waterhouse. He began walking slowly up St. James's Street, scouring his brains for some reasonable solution.

Ten minutes later one had not occurred to him, but he emerged from his reverie to discover himself on the south side of Grosvenor Square. He gave a start, and realized that he had been heading for the very house he had chosen to avoid. He hesitated, thinking afresh. As he reflected, a town carriage with a crest clearly emblazoned on the panel approached at a steady pace and he recognized the carriage of Lady Sherreden. He had barely time to step back against the railings before the carriage passed him and he glimpsed Lady Sherreden in earnest conversation with her mother. He sighed with relief, and continued to walk towards Grosvenor Street.

Even as he stood before number twenty he did not know what to do. Lady Sherreden was out — if Miss Sherreden were at home it would be a splendid opportunity, yet still he hesitated. Afterwards he could not recall what had driven him up those steps, whether it was the thought of Mr. Waterhouse's smile, or some other prompting. In a moment, however he was at the top and impulsively pulling the bell. The servant who opened the door was poker-faced, and had denied both his master and his mistress before the Marquis had even spoken. On his lordship's enquiring particularly for Miss Sherreden, however, a frown puckered his brow for a second before the wooden expression returned.

"If you would care to step inside, my lord, I will see if Miss Sherreden is at home."

Lord Veryan, left alone in the cool, wide hall, gradually became aware of his own reflection in a mirror opposite. Having dressed for his club he was hardly attired for paying his addresses to a young lady of society. The cravat at his throat was carelessly tied, and his hair, having been caught by several buffets of wind on the way, positively untidy. He knew a sudden impulse to fly, but at that moment the servant reappeared, and, with a low bow, prepared to conduct him upstairs. He had barely time to straighten his cravat and run a hand through his disordered locks before a door was thrown open and he heard his own name sonorously announced.

There were two women in the room. One he instantly marked down as a companion. The other, a tall young woman in a plain blue kerseymere gown made high to the throat and buttoned tightly at the wrists was rising to greet him. Lord Veryan was aware of surprise. Against the divine Elizabeth Miss Katharine Sherreden would never show to advantage, but he realized of a sudden that his impression of a slight mousy female was quite wrong. She was, in fact, quite tall, her figure light and pleasing, with her hair, a soft brown, simply arranged about her face. The nose was straight, the mouth firm, and the eyes, at that moment regarding him coolly, a clear grey. He met that gaze, and reddened.

"Lord Veryan," she said in a soft, melodious voice. "I'm afraid both my brother and Lady Sherreden are out, but if you have some message I would be pleased to convey it to them."

"Miss Sherreden," he said, recollecting himself, "I know this will seem most odd, but might I have a word with you in private?" He glanced at the companion, a sharp-featured woman in middle-age.

Miss Sherreden hesitated. She had no idea what this embarrassed young man could want, but since she anticipated no possible danger to her person she turned after a moment and said: "Maria, would you leave us, please. I shall ring if I need you."

The companion, although clearly disapproving, could only roll up her stitchery, and leave. Lord Veryan, wondering what on earth he was at, waited for the door to close before turning to Miss Sherreden. "I know you must think this most odd of me, ma'am — "

"Won't you be seated, my lord?"

He sat, only to stand up at once and start pacing the room. Miss Sherreden regarded him in growing astonishment.

"Miss Sherreden," he said, ceasing his pacing and coming to stand before her, "you must think this very odd, but will you do me the honour of becoming my wife?"

Miss Sherreden's eyes grew large. She began to wonder if he were in his cups. His cheeks were certainly very flushed and his hair could only be called disarranged. On the other hand it was only a little after noon, and it seemed unlikely that he should be inebriated so early in the day. She repressed an absurd desire to laugh. "My lord," she said calmly, "are you quite well?"

He looked at her, and considered how he must appear. A chuckle escaped him. Infinitely easier, he drew a chair nearer to where she sat, and disposed himself in it. "I said you would think it odd, and really I am not at all surprised you think me a trifle disguised, as you clearly do! But I must assure you I am in earnest."

She regarded him appraisingly. "Indeed? If that is so, you will not be offended if I say I really had no idea of what you intended when you entered this room!"

Her easy manner made him relax,

and he grinned at her. "No!" he said, appreciatively. "But now that this is clear, perhaps I ought to explain just why I have made you this offer. It might help you to make up your mind about me."

The grey eyes twinkled. "Perhaps, but I do hope you are not going to say you have formed an attachment for me, for I know it would be untrue!"

"I have a great admiration — " he began, and then met Miss Sherreden's inquiring expression, and faltered. "Oh, dash it all," he said, grinning again, "my grandfather, the Duke of Clayre, wants me to marry. In fact, to be honest with you, Miss Sherreden, he will cut me out of his will if I do not!"

She raised her brows calmly. He had no idea what she was thinking. "What an awkward situation! And you think I would make you a proper wife? Yes, how stupid of me, of course you do otherwise you would not be here, would you, my lord?" She glanced at him surreptitiously, and then looked down at her fingers.

"That's it," he responded gratefully. "The thing is, I have to be married in a trifle of a hurry, and, well, I do know that your — er — situation is not altogether happy."

For a moment she was silent, and he began to wonder if he had gone too far. This proposing was certainly no easy business! Then she sighed, and looked up at him. "You are right, of course. I am merely surprised you have noticed it."

Lord Veryan swallowed. "I am acquainted with both your brother and Lady Sherreden," he managed. "Suffice it to say it has not gone unnoticed."

She nodded thoughtfully. Just how much did she know? "You say at once. Just when is at once?"

He took a breath. "Within one week."

She raised her brows, looked at him consideringly, but said nothing. After a moment she rose and crossed to the long window that looked out over the street. "You have referred to my situation. I will tell you, then, that there is little I would not do to get out of this house. However, I would not do it merely to enter one where a similar life awaits me. Perhaps you would care to tell me just what sort of arrangement you have in mind." She turned now, and lifted her chin a little as she looked at him.

Feeling steadier now, Lord Veryan rose, and approached her. "Naturally it is a marriage of convenience. I would not interfere with you or your pursuits any more than you wish me to. But you never know. Perhaps one day you might come to regard me with some sort of affection."

She nearly laughed then, but somehow controlled it. "Well, I cannot say about that, Lord Veryan. It would all be a matter of time, wouldn't you think? However, as long as you don't fall asleep over the dinner table I don't see why we shouldn't rub along quite well. You don't do that, do you? I really cannot abide people who do such things."

He glanced at her, momentarily deceived, and then caught the twinkle in her eye and grinned. "I shall attempt to reform myself," he promised, "as long as you agree to accept me. Won't you?" The idea of marrying this woman was beginning to appeal to him.

She looked surprised. "Of course! I must admit, the whole business seems highly irregular, but as far as I can see there is no reason why we should not seal our bargain. Will you take wine?" She looked at him inquiringly, and then moved to pull the bell-rope. "Of course, this is highly improper, you know, Lord Veryan. I should not be alone with you, or even entertain you, until you have seen my brother!"

"Well, I know that," he admitted, smiling, "and in fact I never intended to propose to you at all today! It was an impulse, I'm afraid!"

"Was it, indeed! Well, Lord Veryan, I hope you do not intend to go back on your word! There are very serious penalties for such things, you know!"

He grinned. "No, I shan't do that. Besides anything else, I doubt if I could find anyone to marry me in time!"

Miss Sherreden was startled into making a choking noise, but at that moment the servant entered, and it was doubtful whether Lord Veryan heard it.

Some minutes later Lord Veryan was in the street again. His brain reeled. He had acquired himself a lady; she was passably good-looking, and her background was impeccable. There was no money, but really that was unimportant. What had surprised him was his own behaviour in that elegant morning room. Somehow he had been betrayed into revealing far more than he had ever intended, and was now only relieved that he had managed to keep his counsel about that dreadful bet. He had a suspicion that, had she known about it, Miss Sherreden would not have accepted his proposals so readily. But he liked her. He had to admit it, and began to think that they would deal quite well together. He gave a little tug at his cravat and set off towards Grosvenor Square feeling curiously elated. He certainly had not expected to feel like this. Doubtless it was simply because his affairs were settled at last. He would see Sir Robert that evening, but he had no doubt of his acquiescence. Katharine, moreover, was of age. At that corner of Grosvenor Square he hesitated. He felt inclined to return to Boodle's and flaunt his success before his friends, and then he decided that it would hardly be proper before Sir Robert had been informed. On an impulse, therefore, he set off towards Bond Street with the intention of choosing himself a new waistcoat.

4

LORD VERYAN arrived, Sir Robert was agreeable, and Katharine went to bed an engaged woman. She knew she should have been happy, but her heart was unaccountably heavy. She had long been aware of the evils of her situation. What little fortune she had had come to her some six months earlier on her twenty-first birthday, and was not enough even to enable her to live without assistance. She was Sir Robert's half-sister, the daughter of her father's second marriage, and she had been resented by her brother since her birth. Her mother, dying in childbirth, had left her a few hundred pounds. Her father had loved both children dearly, and had hoped, when he died, that by entrusting Katharine to her brother's care until she married he would bring them closer together. It was a forlorn hope. Sir Robert's temper was uncertain, and he disliked his little half-sister. More than ten years had separated them. A large fortune might have reconciled him, but Sir Giles had wasted it, and there had been little to inherit but an estate heavily mortgaged and a number of pressing debts. So he had married. Before the appearance of Elizabeth Katharine's life had been tolerable. Sir Robert saw her as rarely as he could, which suited her very well. But Elizabeth actively disliked her, and their common sex brought them much together. Elizabeth was all Katharine was not, vital, amusing, beautiful, rich. What chance had Katharine when Elizabeth was always there to seize attention and cast her into the shade? She had always thought that she would accept a proposal, any proposal, with alacrity, yet when Lord Veryan had stood before her, offering her what she so desired, she had known a sudden urge to refuse. It was ridiculous, she was well-aware. What was she about even *considering* rejecting a Marquis? He would be a duke one day, then she would be a duchess. Strangely enough, this thought did not occur to Katharine until she lay in bed that night reviewing her good fortune. She laughed at herself. She was utterly mad! It should all have been wonderful, yet it was not. Why?

She did not search her heart for long. She had known it, really, all the time. The reason why it was so awful to have Lord Veryan standing there, proposing marriage, promising not to interfere unless she wished, was that there was no one in the world she would rather marry than Lord Veryan. The interview had been amusing, she had to admit, but all the time there had been a doubt nagging at her mind, something that continually urged her to refuse. Well, she had not, and she had merely herself to thank for it. For a wild moment she had seen, or thought she had seen, what life for them might be like, and it was this, and only this, that had prompted her to accept him. But the situation was a rum one, nevertheless. There had been a time in the not too distant past when she had been almost convinced that Lord Veryan's interests lay in another member of the Sherreden household, but she had never been certain whether he had succeeded or not. If he had, then her position would be an intolerable one. She must simply hope that he had not.

As long as she could persuade her feelings for Lord Veryan to lie dormant she did not think her life would be too unpleasant. There would be money. He could give her whatever she wanted, and there would be balls and parties besides. Everything, in fact, that should make her delirious with happiness. Well, she would be. There was an elegant town house, she knew, in Grosvenor Square. She would be able to entertain, she might even become quite fashionable, and, above all, she would be able to take precedence over

Elizabeth. She could not help chuckling as this thought occurred to her. It was wicked, to be sure, but how angry Elizabeth would be! She wasted a few more minutes on thinking how she would flaunt her new gowns before her sister-in-law and make her unspeakably envious, and then her thoughts became confused, and she drifted into sleep.

During the next few days Katharine had little time to think. She was much involved in preparing for her change in situation, and beyond thinking that Elizabeth seemed curiously unperturbed by the affair she gave little time to reflection. She saw Lord Veryan only once before Friday and that so quickly she hardly realized what was happening before he was gone again. It was perhaps fortunate her time was taken up with preparations and visits, or she might have known some serious misgivings.

Lord Veryan did not. Now that he was resolved and his bride chosen he was actually feeling quite contented.

As far as he could see there was no reason why his life-style should materially alter, although, of course, he would not see Elizabeth, or any other ladies of that sort. He would be obliged to squire Katharine to parties, but he felt he might rather enjoy that. She was, after all, a presentable young woman, and he was hopeful that, when turned out more expensively than at present, she might even do him credit. What was more, he rather thought he liked her. To be sure, she seemed to regard the whole matter somewhat frivolously, but it seemed possible that she might in time come to regard him with a certain fondness. But that was all for the future.

Lord Veryan did not visit his club before the Tuesday. Instead he scribbled four letters to his friends inviting them to St. George's, Hanover Square, at eleven o'clock on Tuesday. He felt their amazement, and grinned as he penned the notes. Then there was his tailor to see, the special licence to buy, the carriage to be ordered, an announcement sent to the 'Gazette'. He had decided to convey his bride directly to Cheard as a sort of honeymoon. The house in Grosvenor Square was to be set in order, and Lord Veryan preferred to be quite out of the way while such business was going on. On Sunday he paid a hurried visit to his betrothed to ask her surreptitiously if she required money to buy her wedding-clothes. It had occurred to him late on Saturday night that it would be just like that purse-pinching Sherreden not to give her a penny. She did not need his help, but had appreciated his kindness, and all the way home he could not help feeling pleased with himself and wondering why it had occurred to him to do such a thing. Perhaps he was becoming responsible at last.

However that was, he needed a little prompting from his man of business before he remembered to collect the family jewels for his bride, or, worse, to buy her a wedding-present. His jaw dropped as he realized the implications of his lapse, and he paid a rapid visit early on the morning of his wedding to Rundell and Bridge to repair this grievous omission. The salesman no sooner gathered the import of the Marquis's visit than he put away the tray of expensive trifles he had drawn out on his lordship's entrance. The Marquis soon discovered that the purchase of a wedding-gift suitable for my lady was a far more sensitive process than his experience had led him to believe, and he was already several hundred pounds the poorer before the salesman lightly inquired whether he also wished to purchase a ring. Covering his dismay as best he could, the Marquis had replied that of course he did, and had been just about to ask. He thought he had carried it off well, but felt severely chastened as he left the establishment with an exquisite string of pearls with matching ear-rings in his pocket, together with a slim and glistening band of gold he was desperately hoping would fit. After that it was something of a rush to get to the church on time, but, although he was pretty sure his bride would not mind if he were late, he naturally preferred his marriage to start well.

He was not late, but he had barely greeted his cronies and handed the ring with an air of pride to Mr. Malling before a glance from the clergyman signified the arrival of his betrothed. He was rather relieved to discover that his bride had forgone her right to yards of satin and lace veil, and was merely becomingly attired in a glisteningly white crepe dress with demi-train, two white roses in her hair and others in a small posy which she clasped with becoming nervousness. The idea that he would be forced to escort a female done up in flowing white all the way to Bath had formed some of his less happy dreams, and he was glad to find that she was, after all, a sensible woman. The ceremony passed off without a hitch. The only guests

73

were Lord Veryan's four friends and Sir Robert and Lady Sherreden. His lordship had contemplated inviting his cousin Edward, the only one of his relations in town. He would have enjoyed seeing his discomfiture, but the recollection that Sir Robert must needs be invited banished the idea. It was sufficient to have one grim and disapproving gentleman at his marriage. There was always the possibility, too, that Sir Edward might not regard the marriage of his cousin with annoyance but instead with glee, and Lord Veryan had no wish to have his relative lauding his triumph in front of his wife. The coach, with the baggage on the roof, arrived on time, and the couple set off without trouble.

The young couple, left alone at last, sat several minutes in silence. Katharine was trying to decide how she really felt about her new life, and Lord Veryan was merely congratulating himself on the smooth running of his preparations. A slim packet had been slipped into his hand by the intermediary, Mr. Malling, as he entered the coach, and this, as much as anything else, contributed to his present satisfaction. Mr. Waterhouse had said very little, merely offering his congratulations, but Lord Veryan had known he was as mad as fire over the whole business, and was probably even now plotting his revenge. Forgetting his wife's existence for a moment, he slipped his hand into his pocket and chuckled, but instead of the packet he had expected, it touched something hard. Mystified, he pulled it out, and remembered the wedding-present he had bought.

"I got this for you," he said casually, grinning as she turned round, surprised. "It isn't much, but you'll have plenty of time to get whatever you want in Bath."

Intrigued, Katharine accepted the box and carefully opened the lid. She stared for a moment at the contents, and then closed it again at looked at her husband. "Indeed, my lord, you should not have done this! You make me feel very guilty. I haven't got you anything!"

Lord Veryan grinned. "Well, to tell the truth, if someone hadn't reminded me I daresay I should have forgotten all about it! I hope you like them, and you really ought to call me Christopher, you know."

"I do like them, very much, and they also happen to be the only jewellery I have! But they are lovely, and I shall call you Christopher."

"I've got the family emeralds packed up somewhere," he said, "and my mother's diamonds if you would rather wear those."

Katharine knew a sudden desire to hug him, but she resisted it, and contented herself with smiling happily. "You really are taking this business seriously, aren't you! Though I suppose you're quite right! Should I put these on now, or would I be overdressed?"

"Put them on. I'd like to see how they look."

"You'll have to fasten them for me, you know. Do you mind?"

Obligingly Lord Veryan took them from her and clasped them about her neck. Her collar hid them, but she could feel them heavy against her throat. She fastened the ear-rings, and turned round for her husband's approval. "Well? Do they look alright?" She watched him eagerly for some indication of his thoughts, but was startled when he suddenly bent forward and kissed her lightly on one cheek. "Well! They must look nice!"

He smiled, and settled back against the squabs. "I was just thinking how lucky I was to have chanced on you, that's all. We should deal very well together."

"Indeed, my lord, I hope so!" She glanced at her husband, then smiled, and relaxed contentedly. "Tell me about your grandfather. Shall I like him?"

He considered her with his head on one side. "I would imagine you would deal famously together. Most people are terrified of him, but he appreciates plain speaking. Yes, I think you'll like him."

She laughed. "You make him sound positively frightening! Do you like him?"

"I admire him, certainly. He's very strong-willed, and generally gets his own way, but he likes a good joke occasionally. He can't bear my cousin, Edward. Calls him a pompous nincompoop."

She chuckled. "And is he?"

"Certainly, though he doesn't think so, of course. As a matter of fact it's his fault grandfather gave me an ultimatum. He reports on me. As soon as the Duke discovered how I passed my time he sent for me. Edward must have been overjoyed. He's had an eye on my position for years. But I daresay you'll find all that out for yourself."

They passed the night at Newbury. The jolting of the carriage had given Katharine a headache she did not need to feign, and even Lord Veryan, after a couple of glasses of bad port, felt the exigences of the day demanded an early night.

They reached Cheard early the following evening. It was a neat house, not large, but admirably designed and laid out. The Duke of Clayre, when still Lord Veryan, had built it for his youthful bride, dismayed by the cold grandeurs of Clayre. Its pretty rooms and neat grounds with woods and lake had exactly suited her.

Katharine, who had felt a little daunted by Lord Veryan's description of his grandfather, was comforted by the sight of such quiet grace and elegance. No one, she felt, who had built such a charming house for his bride could be quite as formidable as his lordship had suggested. The house, barely three miles outside Bath, lay in a valley of its own, and was reached by a long, sweeping drive from the top of the hill. The sun was fast setting as the chaise moved unhurriedly to the front of the house, and the autumn-tinged woods that backed it made it an agreeable picture.

Their arrival had obviously been observed, since the door opened quietly as the carriage came to a halt. A sombrely dressed servant stood waiting, and several uniformed footmen hurried out to open doors and begin removing packages. Katharine was relieved to discover that the immediate introduction had been spared, a message being conveyed to the Marquis to bring his bride to wait on his Grace after dinner.

The meal was a tête a tête affair served in a small dining room by a tall spare servant with greying hair and a slight limp. Lord Veryan, Katharine noticed, called him John, and seemed to be on terms of great friendship. He wore a more benign expression than that usually associated with butlers and other retainers.

"The exact nature of John's position here is rather delicate," explained his lordship as the servant left the room. "He's been with grandfather so many years he's become a sort of general factotum, acting as the Duke's valet as well. He's not particularly tactful with servants, my grandfather," he said, grinning. "He had so many valets you would scarcely believe it, and it gradually became more practical to have John look after him. Of course, he should be called Wilkins, very formally, but for some reason or other he regards the Duke's use of his name as a mark of trust. The other servants would never dare to use it, of course. He's Mr. Wilkins to them! Actually, the Duke makes out it's because of John they're here, though I find that a bit hard to believe. He's supposed to be gouty."

After dinner Katharine, dressed in the only evening gown she possessed, was conducted to another part of the house by her husband. The tastes of a generation before were apparent in the pictures and hangings of the passages but Katharine found herself much in sympathy with the mind that had chosen them. She wished the late Duchess were still alive.

The apartment in which his Grace resided while at Cheard was a wide, high-ceilinged room, dimly lit on this occasion by a single branch of candles set on a table in the centre of the room. Katharine, standing behind her husband in the doorway, thought at first that the room was quite empty, but gradually became aware of an upright figure standing across the room by the curtained windows. After a moment he moved into the centre of the room and she saw that, although his hair and brows were perfectly white, the gentleman bore himself with a straightness that belied Lord Veryan's report of great age. He was, in fact, an elegant old gentleman, dressed with neatness and propriety, and with a definite air of breeding. For a moment he regarded them both from beneath the heavy white brows that almost shrouded his eyes.

"You didn't waste any time, then," he said at last, his expression inscrutible.

"Devil a bit," replied Lord Veryan cheerfully. "Didn't think there was any point in waiting, since you gave me the office. Well, if you don't need me, sir, I think I'll leave you to it. I daresay you'll deal better without me."

His Grace grunted. "Go and amuse yourself with the port, Christopher. I'll ring if I need you."

Lord Veryan grinned at his wife, and then hastened out lest his Grace should change his mind.

"Come and sit over here," said the Duke, his voice suddenly kindlier. "I'll ring for John. Will you drink some wine with an old man?" The tone was gentle, but the glance he cast at her was cool and penetrating.

A smile twitching her lips, Katharine walked calmly towards a chair and contemplated her host with her head on one side. "Now I wonder what answer I should give to that?" she

83

mused, apparently to herself. "Do I say 'Why, sir, you are not old'? But perhaps he does not care for toad-eaters. Should I then put on a shocked expression, thus," she dropped her jaw and opened her eyes wide, "and decline all intoxicating liquor? But that would be hypocritical. Besides, I should care for some wine. No, I am resolved." She raised her chin now, and regarded her host haughtily. "Thank you, your Grace, I shall be very happy to join you."

"Ha! You minx! Go and ring the bell, then!" Katharine smiled and curtseyed, and the Duke allowed an approving twinkle to enter his eyes as she moved across the room. "You are right about one thing," he said, as she joined him again. "If you had tried to toad-eat me I should have sent the both of you packing in the morning, honeymoon or not. Can't abide 'em. Nephew of mine, fellow called Edward, always making up to me. Doesn't do him a bit of good."

Katharine smiled. "I find that not hard to believe!"

"Do you not, indeed! Well you've no mealy-mouthed way about you, that's certain! Bring wine, John. The best claret." The Duke indicated a chair, and lowered himself into a high-backed arm chair not too close to the fire. "So you're Giles Sherreden's daughter. Tell me, was your mother Jane or Maria?"

"Maria, your Grace. Did you know her?"

A slightly thoughtful look entered the blue eyes as he regarded her. "Ay, I knew her. Thought her a vast improvement on that first female he took, too! You've a look of her, sometimes."

"I never knew my mother, but I'm told I resemble her. She was supposed to have a great sense of humour."

The Duke smiled a little absently. "Yes, she had a sense of humour, but she was a beauty, you know. Raven hair." He lapsed into silence, and seemed not to notice when the butler entered with wine and glasses. After a moment, however, he raised his head, and Katharine heard him chuckle softly. "So you decided to marry that cub," he said, pouring two small glasses of wine. "I don't know why. He's got little enough to recommend him but the promise of a dukedom, and he won't have that while I can help it!"

Katharine smiled, and sipped her wine. "From what he said of you, I think he cares more for his grandfather than the title!"

The old man gave a sharp bark of laughter. "That's a mighty pretty way to put it, but I'll wager he said he had no mind to be burdened with the responsibilities! However." He set down his glass and continued to regard her thoughtfully. "If the boy spoke of me at all, he'll have told you I like straight answers. What I want to know is, why did you marry my grandson, and in such a hurry."

Katharine smiled briefly. "Surely you know, your Grace, that any home is better than no home? Well, what little money my mother left me was not enough to let me be independent. My brother housed me, fed me, clothed me, but it was no home."

"You've a steady head, at least. I've heard Robert Sherreden is a pretty loose fish, which will no doubt make you want to eat me."

"I have no illusions about my family, your Grace. Robert always resented me. But to do him justice, it must have been hard, at the age of twelve, to see his mother supplanted in that way, and to have his father's attention divided between him and me."

"Well, you've done your duty by him. Now tell me what you really feel."

Katharine smiled reluctantly. She felt curiously drawn to this blunt old gentleman. "I don't like him, but my life was not unpleasant until he married Elizabeth Slaidburn. I'm afraid I was not all that she thought a dependent sister should be!"

"One of the Slaidburn's, eh? Money, but very little else. Precious little breeding, from what I've heard." He regarded her keenly, but perceived no tell-tale blush. He guessed she did not know, then.

"Robert could have done better, I suppose, but he seems happy enough with the arrangement. I know so little about it."

His Grace of Clayre nodded thoughtfully. "And what of Christopher?" he demanded abruptly. "How will you fare?"

A slight flush crept into Katharine's cheeks as she answered. "Well enough, your Grace. Lord Veryan seems to be an undemanding young man."

"Ay, perhaps too undemanding. Told you you could go your own way, I suppose. Well, I won't pry, but I tell you now, my lady, while I'm head of the family I'll have no scandal attached to the Carradale name!"

There was a quick flash in Lady Veryan's eyes. "Lord Veryan's affairs are of course his own. I shall not interfere where I am not wanted, but if there is any scandal it will be none of my making!"

"Ha! So you've a temper, have you! Well, it won't serve you amiss. I meant no offence, but it's best to know where we stand. You keep Christopher away from the gossips, and I'll be satisfied. He's a good boy, but a little wild. However, I believe he has chosen well."

The sudden and unexpected compliment destroyed all Katharine's powers of speech. She blushed, tried to disclaim, and fell silent.

"Ay, you're a good girl. See he treats you right. He'll run rings round you if he can, and I don't want that, not only for the family's sake!" He considered a moment, then said: "If there's ever any problem, you come to me."

Katharine, who had by now recovered her composure, replied quickly: "Thank you, but I do not anticipate any trouble."

"Then you had better. Christopher's

not a man broke to bridle. He doesn't know what he wants. But you'll teach him. As I say, if there's trouble, come to me, don't go running all over the country to relations you don't like. Come to me. I've a mind to stay here for the winter. Clayre's well enough in its way, but I'm getting no younger, and the wind cuts through that place like a knife."

Katharine smiled then. "Thank you, you are very kind. I shall not forget."

His Grace nodded. "You're a good girl. What do they call you? Kate?"

"Katty, sir."

"Hm, Katty. Unusual, but well enough. Well, Katty, come and shake an old man's hand! We'll deal extremely, you and I!"

5

LORD and Lady Veryan remained three weeks in Bath. His lordship, entering whole-heartedly into his role of husband, conducted his wife all over town, and if he could not be persuaded to go so far as to accompany her to her dressmaker, he managed at least to congratulate her on her taste, and say she looked very well in her new walking-dress. He saw her mounted on one of his Grace's mares, and took her riding in the nearby hills. He told her at once she had a very good seat, soon discovered her to be almost as good in the saddle as himself, and promised handsomely to buy her a mare when they should return to London. He began to think he had chosen very well. Katharine, who looked even finer in her new clothes than he had ever dared to hope, was an uncritical bride, accepting

91

his encomiums on her dress and riding with a smile and a twinkle in her grey eyes. Lord Veryan soon discovered that she was disposed to favour anything he wanted to do, imposed no restrictions on him at all, and even smilingly admitted that there was no reason whatsoever why he should not attend a cock-fight at Bristol though it would take him from her for two days. He began to think that he had done a very handsome thing in giving her a home, and saw no reason why they should not be perfectly happy. To be sure, she was sometimes a little distant, even cold, but she would grow out of that in time. He was in no hurry.

Katharine herself was not discontented. Although his obvious indifference sometimes caused her a pang, he was a fair enough partner, and when she could persuade her feelings to lie dormant she found him very good company. He was an amusing young man, with a knack of knowing just how to please her. But far more often he seemed to forget that she was a woman at all, talking to her much as he would to his friends. She was so unlike the other women of his acquaintance who expected and even demanded his constant flattery and attention, tending to laugh when he paid her extravagant compliments, that he could not avoid speaking to her with greater freedom than he might consciously have done. Contrary to expectation, however, these occasions did not offend Lady Veryan, but rather endeared him to her the more. She found herself generally much in accord with him, and if only her feelings would not keep obtruding themselves on her notice she thought she should be very happy. Even so she passed a very comfortable three weeks. She had dresses that would cheer any female not wholly given over to a monastic existence, and found herself regretting the day that would see them in London.

The Duke of Clayre kept himself as much as possible out of their affairs.

Beyond grunting at the tale of the cock-fight he passed no comment whatsoever on his grandson's behaviour, reflecting that it was up to them to sort their lives out as best they might. The feelings of each had not remained in doubt for long. Lady Veryan was as much in love with her husband as he was oblivious of it, and before they left for London the Duke repeated his offer that she might come to him if she needed help. He was not entirely satisfied with the match. It was painfully obvious that Lord Veryan had all the merit of giving while it was really he who received all that was of value. Katharine's plight worried the old gentleman, and he resolved, therefore, since John's foot seemed no better, to remain at Cheard until the whole business was sorted out.

It was wet for their departure. The weather had been fine, but cold during their stay, but the day before they left the clouds had started gathering overhead, and now they broke on the chaise as they rumbled eastwards. It rained incessantly for almost two days, and although when the coach finally came to a halt outside the impressive front doors of Clayre House, the Carradale family residence in Grosvenor Square, the rain had temporarily ceased, it was a forlorn sight that greeted them. After the fine weather of Somerset, London seemed dull and grey by comparison.

Clayre House was in reality the Duke's town residence. It was, however, rarely used, and his Grace had at once agreed to its being opened up and refurnished for Lord Veryan and his new bride. It was a large and impressive house, and, since Lord Veryan had left the matter of furnishing and staffing it to his man of business it was discovered to be in perfect order and running smoothly. The staff seemed to operate in accord. A bevy of footmen were in attendance as the young couple entered the hall, and if there were the occasional skirmish for supremacy in the servants' hall it was never known above stairs.

The furnishings and hangings chosen by Lord Veryan's agent were quietly elegant, and Katharine, beyond experiencing a slight wish that she had been allowed to choose something for herself, was proud and elated to find herself mistress of so much grandeur. Of course, as time went on she would be able to choose a more becoming shade of pink satin for the chairs in the drawing room, but she was wise enough not to be impatient, and otherwise found everything perfectly satisfactory. There was a moment when it seemed as though the housekeeper would achieve complete supremacy over her mistress, for a rumour, originating from no one knew where, that the new Lady Veryan was a penniless upstart who had been grateful for any home she could get, had rapidly pervaded the lower region of the house. Katharine, however, had a great deal of calm authority, and, after coolly threatening to turn the woman out of her house without more ado unless she learnt to improve her manner, established herself easily as mistress of the establishment. Lord Veryan was a little relieved to discover that his wife apparently knew very well how to run a house and manage the servants. The unpleasant suspicion that he would be obliged to do all that himself had, in fact, occurred to him several times while they were in Bath. Katharine had shown herself to be pleasant, and biddable, and it was nice to find that she was, after all, a very organised and capable young woman. Once again Lord Veryan congratulated himself on his choice.

The rumour, however, seemed, during the absence of the Marquis and his bride, to have spread to quite different quarters. Katharine had made her appearance in society, such as it was, some years previously, and had thereafter been politely ignored by one and all. Now, however, several spurned maidens and their mamas discovered that they had always known Katty Sherreden to be a scheming and encroaching female, and this action of stealing one of the largest prizes on the marriage mart merely confirmed them in this opinion. Several came to pay their respects and to see how vulgarly she would conduct herself, and while Katharine was never at a loss to account for the sudden increase in her acquaintance, she was obliged to choke back several very hot retorts in answer to their insolence. Some visitors, however, came out of kindness, particularly those who had known her mother years before, and one, Lady Sefton, to offer her the prized and coveted vouchers for Almack's. For in spite of her former penniless condition Katty Sherreden had always been 'bon ton', and her breeding was impeccable. Generally, therefore, she found herself very well accepted, if not for what she had been, or even was, then certainly for what she would one day become.

Altogether Katharine was enjoying herself very well. She wasted no time in setting about cutting a dash, and when she had visited a Bond Street dressmaker and had ordered herself several very expensive gowns, began to feel very much more up to snuff. Elizabeth had been one of her earliest callers, and had so excited Katharine's envy by the splendour of her walking dress, and the hat with feathers that stroked her cheek, that she had at once resolved to give all her old gowns to the housekeeper. Lord Veryan regarded her extravagances with indulgence. He could, after all, afford to be generous, and besides this it gave him an odd feeling of contentment to make Katharine happy. Only once was he a little startled by his wife's desires, and this had been more out of anxiety for her safety than from any sense of meanness.

When she had first told him, he had thought she was joking, and had laughed cheerfully across the breakfast table. No sooner was it borne in upon him that she was serious, however, than he began to have misgivings.

"A phaeton?" he echoed. "You, Katty? Surely you aren't serious! Why, you can't even drive!"

"How do you know that? I might drive very well!"

He raised his brows at her. "Do you, then?"

"Yes. As a matter of fact, my lord, I used to be quite skilled. Father taught me. He taught both of us, you know, and Robert is a member of the Four Horse Club."

This was deliberate provocation. For several years Lord Veryan had been trying to become a member of this exclusive club, but had still to find someone irresponsible enough to nominate him. "The fact that Robert can handle the ribbons means nothing at all, as well you know! How can I have my wife dashing about the town being a danger to herself and all who come near?"

"Why don't you try me, my lord," suggested Katharine, her lips twitching slightly. "With you up beside me to catch the ribbons if I should falter how can I go wrong?"

And so she had prevailed. Two days later Katharine, having handled her husband's pair to perfection, was reluctantly escorted to the appropriate warehouse for the selection of a suitable vehicle. But here, too, a problem arose. Lord Veryan was, by this time, resigned to buying his wife an elegant phaeton of the type generally favoured by ladies of the ton. He had not been there for many minutes, however, before he became aware that the carriages at which Lady Veryan was looking were hardly what might be described as elegant. A perilous vehicle, one of the high-perch variety with the body, quite five feet off the ground, poised directly above the front axle seemed to have caught her fancy. Having shut his eyes for a moment in horror Lord Veryan opened them to discover his wife on the point of closing the deal with the salesman. A few hurried words had done little to dissuade her, and he had been forced to draw her aside and conduct a whispered argument under the full observation of the salesman.

"I cannot imagine what you are thinking of!" he exclaimed throbbingly, casting a surreptitious glance over his shoulder. "You will turn it over at the slightest provocation!"

Katharine raised her brows and smiled. "Really, Christopher, why are you so distressed? I thought you had agreed to my purchasing a phaeton."

"A phaeton, yes, but not that . . . that monstrosity!"

"Oh, do you think it ugly? If that is your objection then I suppose it might well be valid, but after all, Christopher, you will not be obliged to travel in it!"

"You are deliberately misunder-standing me! You know very well that such a vehicle is dangerous unless handled by the very best whip!"

She looked blandly up at him. "I wasn't suggesting you drive it, my lord."

For a moment she thought he would explode, then suddenly his face relaxed and he gave a reluctant smile. He was, in fact, finding it harder and harder to refuse her anything. "Do you really think you can handle it?"

"I'm not an idiot, Christopher, you know. Surely you know I would not even contemplate buying such a thing if I were not perfectly confident I would be safe?"

Lord Veryan was silent for a moment, his brow puckered as he looked down at her. "You really want it?"

She bit her lip and nodded, her eyes shining excitedly like a child's. He could not resist her. Shaking his head and smiling, he crossed to the salesman and closed the deal with him.

"You won't do anything foolish, Katharine, will you?" he said, as they left the warehouse a few minutes later.

She smiled engagingly up at him. "I will undertake, my lord, to be very careful. There is one thing, though, that I thought I might do."

He looked at her inquiringly.

"I understand it is quite a feat to drive down St. James's Street."

She deceived him completely. A few yards from the carriage Lord Veryan stopped dead, and regarded his wife with an expression of horror. "My God!" he exclaimed hoarsely. "I must have been mad!"

Lady Veryan looked at him interestedly. "To do what, my lord? Marry me, or buy the phaeton?"

"Both!" he responded explosively.

Katharine laughed then, and took his arm affectionately. "You must think me very dreadful, Christopher! Did you really believe I would do such a thing? How unkind I am! I give you my word, my lord, that I will not go within one street of St. James, and will confine myself to driving at a sedate trot around the park."

"Upon my word, Katty, you worried me! You won't do it, will you, even as a joke?"

"No, my lord, I promise."

He sighed with relief. "Thank the Lord for that," he said, and handed her into the carriage.

Thus Katharine was pretty well satisfied with her new situation, and if she was a little perplexed by her sister-in-law's attitude, well, it was nothing to be concerned about.

Elizabeth had paid her wedding visit early. Katharine had expected her to call, and had even been prepared to see her pleased that she was no longer obliged to house her, but quite unexpected was Lady Sherreden's air of quiet triumph. This was a complete mystery. For some reason Elizabeth believed she had won a victory over her sister-in-law, and for this Katharine was at a loss to account. That she should be glad Katharine was married was understandable, but the new Lady Veryan had expected to see signs of rage and envy that one whose prospects had been so poor should elevate herself so quickly. It was a complete puzzle. She attempted to put it out of her mind, but it taunted her again as she lay in bed that night. She recalled a suspicion she had harboured some months before her marriage, that Lord Veryan had been very interested in Elizabeth, and it occurred to her to wonder whether he had in fact succeeded. But even this would not account for Elizabeth's satisfied air, and she resolved to think of it no more.

Lord Veryan's contentment with his new situation showed no signs of a rapid abatement. He visited his club just as often as before, and received his friends' congratulations and jokes with evident satisfaction and unfailing good humour. When the general amazement of the members about his sudden marriage had subsided his friends seemed resigned to his fate, only Mr. Waterhouse showing any kind of scepticism about the affair. The others agreed, however, that this was generally to be expected, considering the substantial sum of money that had changed hands, although one or two did wonder what Mr. Waterhouse was plotting by way of revenge. The Marquis wondered too, but it did not occur to him to worry. He felt confident now of being able to deal with whatever challenge Mr. Waterhouse set him.

It was not long, however, before any excitement raised by the Marquis of Veryan's sudden marriage was smothered by a rush of interest in a second robbery, performed in a manner strikingly similar to that which had affected the capture of the Winslow rubies. The event, however had a startling twist. Sir John Timpson, summoned to a visitor who awaited him in his library, was surprised to find the room plunged in darkness. An ejaculation had barely escaped him before he was caught round the neck from behind in a strong grasp while a second character seized a valuable diamond pin from the folds of his cravat, and both escaped through the window which had been opened in readiness. So astounded had

Sir John been that it was a few seconds before he could call for aid. By the time the candles had been relit, a man sent to scour the gardens and another to summon the Watch, the villains had quite disappeared. It seemed Sir John was vastly upset by his loss. The pin had been an heirloom, handed down through several generations, an intricate design of stars and moons upon which no price could be placed. As usual the servant who had admitted the thief could recall little about him. The card he had produced had been inscribed John Davis, Esq., and the gentleman himself was merely tall, slim with brown hair and an ordinary expression.

"I see how it is," pronounced Mr. Barton gloomily. "They'll be murdering us as we sleep soon, mark me."

"Lord, Bart," said the Marquis irritably, "What would they want to do that for? It's the valuables they want, and dashed clever they are about getting them."

"Think it's the same people, Ver?"

asked Mr. Malling, interestedly.

"Sure to be. Same cool method. I tell you this, Freddie, I wish I'd thought of it, indeed I do! Would have saved a deal of trouble!"

"Come, come, Ver, dear boy!" exclaimed Mr. Malling, rolling his eyes heavenwards. "Fine woman, Lady Ver, couldn't do better!"

"Dash it, Freddie," exclaimed Lord Veryan, horrified. "I'm not talking about her la'ship! Couldn't have done better if I'd tried! No, what I mean is, what a good lark, Freddie! Cunning, I call it."

Mr. Waterhouse took snuff.

Speculations as to the identity of the thieves were rife, one theory being that it was a band made up of present and past servants of the ton, since the habits of the victims appeared to be very well-known. Other theories were suggested, but this was the one that found most favour, and employers in fashionable London began looking askance at their staff.

"I think the suggestion that a member of the ton is responsible is quite ludicrous," stated the formidable Lady Petrie to her spouse one evening. "Of course it is a servant. Who else would stoop to such a base and cunning method of obtaining money?"

"Members of the ton are just as dependent on money as the serving classes," remarked her spouse mildly. "In my opinion the thefts smack of the effrontery and daring some of our young men abound in today."

"Nonsense," snapped his wife, and the subject was dropped.

Lord Veryan continued to regard the thefts as a very good lark, and looked forward with interest to when the next one should be perpetrated. Katharine, however, whose few pieces of jewellery were immensely valuable to her since they were of such recent acquisition, could not but be nervous about it, and told her husband as much. As first he was inclined to laugh, but, when he saw she was in earnest, had merely pinched her cheek and told her not to worry. If she lost any piece he would simply buy her another. This was not quite the assurance Katharine had wanted, and instead of comforting her had made her feel even more uneasy. It seemed her husband was half-expecting her to be robbed. He clearly did not worry, however, so she told herself she was making a fuss about nothing, and should regard her possessions as casually as her husband apparently did. If this was not quite possible, she put on a creditable appearance of unconcern, and Lord Veryan was pleased to see that his words had apparently allayed her fears. It relieved him, for he was having troubles of quite another order.

When he had married Katharine he had been perfectly aware of how it would seem in the eyes of Lady Sherreden. He had hoped, however, that by being demonstrably cooler when next they met that she would realize he had no intention of returning to the cosy and comfortable relationship they had once enjoyed. It had not taken many days for him to realize that this was a forlorn hope. Lord Veryan was not one to abstain from all rational enjoyment simply because his one-time mistress was to be present. It would take far more than that to make him cry off. But she seemed always to be present at the balls, and parties, at Almack's, at the Opera and the Play. What was more, she was always obtruding herself on his notice. He did not feel Katharine suspected, although she was clearly surprised that her sister-in-law should suddenly take so much interest in her, but then, what should be more natural than that they should often be together? Nevertheless, it could not but make Lord Veryan uneasy, and he wished Lady Sherreden would adopt a less familiar form of speaking to him when Katharine was present. She seemed determined to convey the impression to Lady Veryan that she and the Marquis shared a secret from which Katharine was excluded, and Lord Veryan felt that, if Katharine did not guess from Lady Sherreden herself, he would be likely to betray them by his own nervous and peculiar behaviour.

Katharine did notice, but she noticed too that her husband was doing his best, for whatever reason, to repulse the lady, and she could not prevent herself from smiling a little that her sister-in-law's attempts to steal her husband should be so thwarted. Whatever his lordship's feelings had once been, she felt that now they were nothing other than they should be. It would not be long, she thought, before Lady Sherreden would be obliged to look elsewhere for her amusement.

Had it been simply as Katharine deduced, no doubt Lady Sherreden could soon have got tired of such a cool reception, but Katharine was not aware of what had passed between the Marquis and Lady Sherreden at Lady Jefford's ball. Lord Veryan remembered it, and it caused him a little loss of sleep. He began to fear that Elizabeth, finding herself thwarted, would reveal to her sister-in-law just why he had married her, and this, above all else, he wished to avoid.

It was this very fact that caused Elizabeth to be complacent. She had no doubt of her power over the Marquis, for who, after all, could prefer mouse-brown locks and cool grey eyes to golden curls and the most limpid blue eyes one had ever seen? She was prepared for a little struggle, indeed she welcomed it, for it would make the capitulation all the sweeter. It annoyed her just a little to see Katharine so calm, but there was time enough. Consequently one afternoon, about a month after the Marquis and his bride had returned from Bath, she paid a call in Grosvenor Square at a time when she knew perfectly well that Katharine would be out — she had an appointment with her dressmaker — and that Lord Veryan would be alone.

At first the man-servant was inclined to refuse her. Lady Veryan was out, he said.

"I know that very well," said Lady Sherreden in proprietary accents. "I should like to see my brother-in-law, if you please, Lord Veryan."

Her manner was so assured that the servant, after hesitating a moment longer, stepped back, and bowed her into the hall. He had opened the door to the library and announced her before Lord Veryan had the slightest idea she was in the house.

His dismay was palpable. He had been idly flicking through a pile of accounts on his desk, and several papers hung in his fingers as he stared aghast at the vision in blue. The click of the door behind the servant brought him to his senses, and he returned the papers to the desk with a gesture of annoyance.

"My dear Christopher," said Elizabeth, calmly drawing off her gloves, "you do not seem very pleased to see me! I had thought you would have been delighted!"

"Dash it, Elizabeth," he exclaimed, scraping back his chair and standing up at last, "you thought no such thing! You know perfectly well you should not be here!"

She gave a tinkly laugh. "Dear Christopher, whyever not? I am your sister-in-law, you know, or had you forgot?"

"I had not, but you ought to know I had been trying to!"

She seated herself elegantly in a soft leather chair and smiled invitingly. "Dearest Christopher!" she said soothingly. "You must not think that because we are now related we can no longer see each other! Why, it makes it almost proper!"

He took hasty strides across the room. "That was not what I meant, as you know! How dare you come here when Katharine is out? What will people say? You know what servants are, always on the look-out for gossip! If this comes to Katharine's ears, Elizabeth, I shall personally choke the life out of you!"

"Dear, dear! So violent! Come, Christopher, this is not like you! Have you forgotten already what we discussed? How we decided it would be the very thing for us now that your horrid cousin was talking about you?"

"No, I have not forgotten, Elizabeth, and I believe I never shall! I'll have you know I did not marry Katharine for that reason."

Elizabeth stood up now, and moved towards him as he stood leaning against the book-shelves. Anger burning in his eyes, he watched her approach, then, as she reached him and turned her enormous blue eyes up to his he laughed suddenly, and flicked her cheek with a careless finger.

"Dash it, Lizzy, you're an unprincipled hussy! You know very well I don't want you!"

Elizabeth smiled up at him. "Do I! It doesn't seem that way to me, my

lord! You look just the same as ever!"
She raised one small white hand to
his face and gently stroked his cheek.
For a moment he stared down at her,
his mind a blank, conscious only of
her scent and the invitation in her
eyes. Then, of a sudden, he recollected
himself, and pushed her roughly away.

"Damn you, Elizabeth, what are you
thinking of? Please leave! Katharine
will be home directly!"

Lady Sherreden, pretty well satisfied,
gathered her gloves from the desk and
unhurriedly drew them on. He was
hers, she knew. Katharine had not
penetrated that casual exterior. She
would go now, but she had every
intention of returning.

Lord Veryan did not look at her
again. His own defection horrified him,
for he had been dangerously near to
clasping her in his arms and forgetting
all about his patient bride. He had
not thought himself so weak as to
succumb to her first attempt. Hearing
the front door close firmly, he heaved

a sigh, and returned slowly to his desk. Accounts and bills littered the surface, but did not hold his attention. What had, until now, been a vague fear, suddenly took on very real proportions, and he had no idea how to face his problem.

A slight sound penetrated his thoughts, and he looked up quickly. Katharine was there, smiling at him, a picture of happiness and complacency. "Good day! Have I disturbed you? You seemed very engrossed, I must say! Was it something enthralling?"

Trying to banish the guilt in his mind Lord Veryan smiled and stood up hastily. "It's nothing, merely bills. A matter of necessity, I'm afraid."

She wrinkled her brow. "My goodness! Are we in debt already?"

He smiled then. "No, of course not. I am trying to be a model husband, Katharine, and keep account of how much we spend."

The grey eyes widened. "Good gracious, Christopher, you have changed!

I'm sure you were never so wont to be so steady!"

He smiled ruefully. "That's too true, I'm afraid. Still, I have hopes we may remain solvent now."

"I certainly wish we may!" She smiled, and drew off her gloves. As she laid them on the table a lingering whiff of Elizabeth's scent caught her nostrils and she sniffed in delight. "What lovely perfume! Have we had a visitor?"

Lord Veryan blenched at once. He attempted a laugh. "No, of course not! What makes you think so? I expect it is the flowers in the hall."

Katharine looked at him a moment. "Of course," she said at last. "That is what it must be. Well, my lord, since you seem to be so occupied, I will disturb you no longer." Calmly she gathered her gloves, and with a slight smile left the room.

The Marquis sat down heavily. What a fool he was! Why had he not told her the truth? Like as not she knew it was Elizabeth's perfume, and what would she think now? He was an imbecile not to trust her, to tell her Lady Sherreden had called. Why should she suspect anything unless he gave her a hint? Well, he had now, of that he was sure. He sighed, and drummed his fingers on the surface of the desk. He certainly was not adept at keeping out of trouble. That was sure!

Katharine mounted the stairs thoughtfully. Strange and totally unwelcome suspicions were arising, and refused to be banished. It was not merely that the flowers in the hall had died and been removed that morning. She knew very well to whom that scent belonged, and had been on the point of saying so when something had stopped her. An unmistakeable look of guilt had passed over her husband's face, and gave rise to suspicions that would otherwise have lain dormant. Gaining her chamber Katharine became aware of a sensation hitherto unknown. She felt a sudden and burning desire to take Elizabeth's slim neck between her fingers and slowly choke the life from her. Paling a little Katharine sat down suddenly on the bed. The realisation of the jealousy she felt made her weak at the knees, and she ran one shaky hand across her eyes. She had always suspected that something had existed between her husband and her brother's wife, but had, until now, chosen to believe that whatever had been between them had ended on her marriage. It seemed this was not so and another suspicion, even more unwelcome than the first, could not but occur to her. The marriage had brought Elizabeth and the Marquis so often together that it could not be discounted as imagination. She stood up and crossed with hurried steps to the dressing table. That the Marquis should take her, Katharine Sherreden, for his wife simply to be near her sister-in-law was unthinkable and unbearable. Her fingers, white and strained, closed firmly round a small jar on the dressing table and gripped it tightly. Turning suddenly, she hurled it across the room against the opposite wall where it shattered at once, and slowly dripped its contents down the paper and on to the carpet. Katharine, white-faced and horrified, sank to the floor in a heap.

6

IT was some time before Katharine could calm herself sufficiently to stand up, and then it was only the recollection that her maid, Ellie, could come upon her at any moment that made Katharine collect her thoughts and get to her feet. She made a rather inexpert attempt to clean up the mess on the wall and carpet, but she removed the broken jar, and decided to leave the rest to the maid. The burning jealousy and resentment gradually subsided into a calm and ordered hatred for Elizabeth and a determination not to let her husband see how much he had humiliated her. She was at first a little shocked to find such violent emotions within her, then she laughed bitterly as she thought of the acute dislike with which Elizabeth had regarded her for some little time.

She resolved at that moment to two things; first, to outwit Elizabeth in any way she could, and second, to make her husband see plainly and clearly just what he was in imminent danger of throwing away.

It was some time, sitting on the bed, before Katharine recollected just what her present activities should be. On returning from her dressmaker she had had a little over half an hour before she needed to change for dinner, but now, if she did not immediately make haste, she was in danger of being late. Pulling the bell hastily, she set about removing her maltreated bonnet, then started struggling with the awkward fastenings to her gown. Ellie, entering a few minutes later, found her mistress contorting herself to reach a button in the small of her back, and could not help giggling as she came forward to help.

"My lady, you are in a hurry! I declare you'll never get that button undone like that, unless you pull it off, o'course!"

Katharine smiled reluctantly, and turned her back to the maid with a creditable show of patience. This nearly stopped when the maid seemed to be taking over-long with her fastenings but at last the gown fell to the floor and she was able to step out of it. Ellie, regarding her mistress from beneath her pale lashes, was rather surprised to see her ladyship biting her lip agitatedly, and then reflected that it was none of her business anyway. Wordlessly, she encouraged her mistress into the low stool and began removing the pins from Lady Veryan's coiffure.

Katharine stared at herself discontentedly. The face that looked back at her was well enough, she supposed, but it would never be other than ordinary. The hair, a soft brown, curled quite freely and generally shone healthily when brushed, but her nose was too thin, and her chin, unfortunately, rather too determined. Expressive grey eyes were doubtless all very well, but what chance did they stand against those of a heavenly blue? Katharine shut her eyes, but when she opened them again the picture was just the same. She made a resolution.

Her salvation did not lie in her looks. That was clear. It must lie, then, in her nature and her behaviour. She took a breath, and considered herself speculatively. She was altogether too weak, too willing to be dominated. It was not that her nature was not strong; she could be very determined when she wished, and had several times been known to lose her temper. No, it was with one person only that she was weak, and he was the one person who must think her strong.

Ellie's agile fingers were busy on Katharine's head, and soon an elaborate arrangement began to take shape. It was a style that Katharine favoured, and one which she had used several times, and now it was more than half finished before she made a gesture to her maid.

"Ellie, I'm sorry, you are doing very

well, but could we have something different for tonight? It is Lady Cheveley's ball, and I want to look particularly well."

Ellie stifled a sigh, and considered the reflection speculatively. Then, under her mistress's watchful eye, she brushed out the elaborate curls that had adorned Katharine's head and began to smooth the hair across her brow. As she commenced the new style she reflected that if only her mistress had mentioned it earlier she would have been happy to do something different. The arrangement of curls was very well, but it lacked the air of simplicity that characterised the young ladies of the day. Now she twisted the hair into a simple knot on the top of Katharine's head, and encouraged the short ringlets to fall down and over the ears. Katharine watched this operation doubtfully. She was afraid it would make her look too young, but the result was, in fact, quite different. She looked unlike herself. Quite pretty, as it happened. She nodded her approval, therefore, and stood up for her dress.

It was new and she had never worn it before. It had been made especially to set off the Carradale emeralds, and was of a deep, glistening gold, slashed open over an unexpected under-dress of rich green. It was quite plain, designed to show off the beauty and fire of the family jewels. Ellie opened the box reverently, and took the heavy necklace from its cushioned bed. It was fashioned like a collar, the fine stones interspersed with a filigree pattern in gold. It was very beautiful, and lay cold and glistening against Katharine's throat as Ellie fastened the clasp.

"It seems a bit stiff, my lady," the maid remarked as she fiddled with the clasp. "There! You won't lose it, at any rate. I thought for a minute it wasn't going to do, but it's right enough now."

"Thank you, Ellie. I should have had it checked, I suppose, when the Marquis gave them to me. But you say it will be alright for tonight?"

"Oh yes, my lady, though we may have a little trouble in getting them off!"

"Well, I'd rather have it that way than lose them!" Katharine remarked with a smile. "Thank you, Ellie, you've been very patient."

The maid bobbed, and ventured to say how fine her mistress looked.

"Well, I hope so, indeed! Have you my gloves and reticule?"

Katharine was in the drawing room before her husband. He had lingered over-long in the library, and from a certain reluctance to meet his wife kept her waiting nearly half an hour. When he appeared he seemed flushed, but Katharine gave no sign of having noticed, and complimented him cheerfully on his dress.

He smiled, momentarily diverted. "Well, I should think it might look fine, considering the time it took me to tie my cravat! However, I think it is well enough now." He paused, and seemed to notice her appearance for the first time. He stared at her a moment, laughed awkwardly, and lowered himself into a chair, taking care not to crease the tails of his coat. "Green suits you," he said abruptly, searching in his pocket for his snuff box. "That's not one of your Bath dresses is it?"

Katharine laughed lightly. "No. Do you like it? I had it made especially for this necklace, and I must admit I think it looks well."

The Marquis agreed and they fell silent. Katharine was anxious not to appear troubled, but no topic of conversation suggested itself, and she was glad when, not long afterwards, dinner was announced. Once she had something to concentrate on, namely the consumption of her meal, she found herself able to maintain a surprising amount of small-talk, and the meal passed without awkwardness. The Marquis seemed a little strained, but Katharine gave no sign of noticing anything.

They arrived in Mount Street a little after ten to join the steady stream of guests. Katharine found her attention claimed almost at once by Lady Lovegrove, and did not hesitate to leave her husband's side. She felt him staring after her, then he moved slowly across the room and out of view. Katharine was determined to enjoy herself, but it seemed occasionally like an up-hill struggle. Lady Lovegrove was enthusiastic about Katharine's necklace. It seemed her mother had told her how beautiful it was but she had never yet had a chance to see it.

"I believe the late Duchess was the last person to wear it," said Katharine, smiling, "and that was many years ago. Lord Veryan's mother was, of course, never in a position to own them, dying before the Duchess herself."

Lady Lovegrove nodded. "Very sad. Still, my dear, they look very well on you." She linked her arm in Katharine's in a familiar fashion and began walking down the room. "I myself have some lovely pearls, quite fine, they are, but one hesitates to wear these things now, doesn't one? Of course, I thought of having a copy made of the necklace and wearing that out, but naturally that would not protect one at all, since one could hardly go about telling one's friends one's jewels were not real!" She laughed cheerfully. "Oh well, I expect we have heard the last of this nasty stealing business, don't you? With all the Runners out and everyone on their guard he would hardly risk his hand now, would he?"

"Well, I certainly hope not! Lord Veryan said if I lost mine he would buy me some more, but I don't think he'd be very pleased if it came to it!" She smiled. "From what I see, people are not really paying much attention to the robberies. Lady Jefford is wearing the most beautiful diamond necklace I have ever seen!"

"She doubtless thinks she is now

exempt," drawled a voice behind them. Katharine swung round. Mr. George Waterhouse, severe in black, was returning his quizzing glass to his pocket and regarding them with a slight smile. "Lady Lovegrove! Lady Veryan! How delightful to see you!"

Lady Lovegrove laughed and blushed, but Katharine could never be certain when he was serious. Her eyes twinkled at him as she said: "Why, sir, how nice of you to say so!"

He laughed then, and, with a nod to Lady Lovegrove, who had suddenly been caught by a passing acquaintance, drew Katharine away. "Your husband has deserted you early, I see! How very poor of him!"

Katharine smiled, but said: "Indeed, sir, I hope I am not a wife to keep my husband permanently at my side! I am sure he may do as he pleases!" Her words were light, but Mr. Waterhouse was quick to catch the bitter inflection, and glanced sharply at her.

"He will not be monopolizing you

in the dancing, then," he said bowing gravely to a passing lady.

She laughed. "Naturally not! In fact, I should be very much surprised if he dances with me at all!"

"Then, my lady, I shall claim the honour of your hand. I certainly cannot leave you to sit out the opening set. You are far too fine for such a thing!"

Katharine thanked him, but her colour rose, and she was glad when he changed the subject.

"Now why is Carradale staring at us, I wonder? I am beginning to think there is something wrong with my coat, though what, I can't imagine!"

Katharine looked up quickly, and Sir Edward, catching her eye, instantly turned away. "Oh, he's a cousin, you know. I expect he will now tell his Grace how friendly we seemed to be!"

Mr. Waterhouse looked astonished. "Does he really report on you in that way? I wonder Lord Veryan stands for it!"

"He would dearly love to see the

back of him, believe me! He expresses himself as wanting to plant him a facer! I believe that is the term?"

Mr. Waterhouse chuckled. "It is indeed! And I don't blame him, either! But tell me, does the Duke believe everything he hears?"

"Oh no, at least, I don't think so, though there have been occasions, according to Lord Veryan, when he caused some very bad feeling between them."

"That I can well believe," Mr. Waterhouse spoke thoughtfully, his eye on the rotund figure across the room. Then he smiled, and extended his arm. "Come, my lady. Shall we join the set?"

The Marquis of Veryan watched all this in growing discontent. It was not that he did not like his friends to be kind to his bride. Indeed, it gave him a sense of pride and pleasure to see them taking trouble over her. What bothered him was the proprietary way in which Mr. Waterhouse had drawn her apart, and, later, had conducted her to the set. What was more, he had seemed very pleased with her. Katharine too had looked happy. He sighed, and tried to attend to Mr. Malling. But the attempt was vain, and soon his attention was wandering again. It returned with a jump after a moment when he discovered Lady Sherreden at his side, smiling up at him.

"In a brown study, my lord?" she inquired softly. "How unlike you, indeed!"

Lord Veryan looked down at her unsmilingly. "What do you want, Elizabeth?"

The blue eyes widened. "Why, my lord, so ungracious? Will you not dance with me?"

"No, I will not," responded his lordship bluntly. "And you should know better than to suggest it."

"Indeed, my lord, I do not understand you! Do you not mean to dance at all? I declare Lady Veryan seems to have no such qualms."

The Marquis's smooth brow darkened. "Meaning just what, Elizabeth?"

She laughed lightly. "Oh, my lord, my lord, so grave! She is enjoying herself, my dear!"

Something stirred in Lord Veryan's unquiet mind. Across the room Katharine was laughing, her head held high, the green stones flashing against the white of her neck. Mr. Waterhouse was smiling down at her in a very familiar way. Lord Veryan's gaze came back to Elizabeth, still looking up at him invitingly. "Very well," he said curtly, "but this once only."

She took his arm immediately, and led him onto the floor. Katharine, who had managed throughout to keep her spouse under observation, became more lively as a result.

Mr. Malling was puzzled. "What's Veryan playing at?" he demanded of his companion. "He should know better than to dance with Lady Sherreden in full view of all the tattle-mongers."

Mr. Barton looked on gravely.

"Dashed if I know. Foolish business all round. Bound to get back to Lady Ver this way. Always does."

"Thing is," said Mr. Malling pensively, "I thought he'd finished with her ladyship. Best thing to do, but it seems I'm wrong."

Mr. Barton nodded, and the two fell silent.

Katharine laughed again and glanced across at her husband. He had his back to her, but Lady Sherreden was plainly visible and seemed to be enjoying herself hugely. She made a point of smiling charmingly up at her companion.

Lord Veryan was scowling. In spite of Lady Sherreden's constant smiles he was finding it difficult to throw off his ill-humour, and occasional glimpses of his happy wife did little to assist him. As the dance brought them together Lady Sherreden said confidingly: "My lord, she will think you are jealous if she sees you looking so black!"

It was a good ploy. Lord Veryan's

139

jaw dropped, and he looked thoughtful. Consequently, when the dance gave Lord and Lady Veryan a clear view of each other again, each managed to convey the impression that they were managing perfectly well, thank you, with their present partner.

The refreshments were laid out in a room at one end of the ball room, and thither Mr. Waterhouse conducted his fair partner when the dancing was finished. Thither too Lord Veryan ushered Lady Sherreden, with the single purpose of keeping his wife in view. Lady Sherreden, on whom the Marquis's intention was not lost, was none too pleased at being forced to pursue her sister-in-law, and therefore stopped before the entrance to the refreshment room and confronted his lordship.

"Really, Christopher, I had not thought you could be so ungallant! You may bring me a glass of champagne. I shall wait for you here."

Lord Veryan, who was not loth to

leave his partner outside, nodded in agreement, and entered the refreshment room alone.

When he wished to be, Mr. Waterhouse was a very entertaining gentleman, and Katharine, in spite of thinking every moment of someone else, was nevertheless diverted by his cool wit. The smile she gave him, therefore, as her husband entered the room, was perfectly spontaneous and charming. Lord Veryan felt his temper rise.

"Damn the fellow," he thought irately. "He's too familiar by half! First he makes me marry her, now he tries to steal her from under my nose!" He took a purposeful step forward, but at that moment Mr. Waterhouse looked up, and the Marquis hesitated. Then Mr. Waterhouse turned to Katharine, said something Lord Veryan could not hear, and with a smile moved away. Katharine turned now and faced her husband. The laugh had died, and she regarded him with a distinct challenge in her eyes. She raised her chin as he approached her with hasty steps, then raised her glass to her lips and contemplated him over the rim.

"Why, my lord," she said as he reached her, "are you here? I hope you have not worried about me, for I have been well attended to by one of your friends."

Lord Veryan was inclined to argue over this epithet, but the room was crowded, and he merely removed the glass from her hand and set it back on the table. Then, drawing her arm within his, he conducted her back to the ball room.

Katharine was not displeased by this calm assertion of ownership, but the effect was somewhat marred by Lady Sherreden, who exclaimed as they entered the ball room:

"Why, there you are, my lord! I declare I have been waiting this age for you! Did you remember my champagne?"

Lord Veryan looked fulminous, but Katharine slipped her hand from beneath her husband's arm and said smilingly: "You should not neglect your partner, Christopher. I am quite alright. Lord Veryan will attend to you now, Elizabeth." Upon which words she smiled at them both and moved away, leaving neither with very charitable feelings towards her.

"Curse you, Lizzy, what did you want to interfere for? There are plenty of gentlemen present who would be only too pleased to serve you."

"I daresay, but what do I want with them? Indeed, my lord, I am sorry if I said a wrong thing, but Katty seemed to be getting on so well with Mr. Waterhouse that I really did not expect to see her on your arm the next minute!" She smiled engagingly at him.

For a moment Lord Veryan stared down at her. "Well, I daresay you meant no harm, after all. Come, I'll get you your wine."

By about half an hour later Lord Veryan finally managed to rid himself of Lady Sherreden by surrendering her to an eager-eyed young buck who came to claim her hand. He cast his eyes around the company for his wife, and found her in a moment in earnest conversation with her host, Lord Cheveley. He was an inoffensive gentleman, but one with a reputation for an eye for a pretty face, and Lord Veryan found himself not a little incensed. It was not enough for his wife to hob-nob with his worst enemy — not that she knew him for that, he conceded fairly — she must now blatantly encourage the oldest flirt in the room to dangle after her in that odious way. He strode across the room towards her and presented himself at her side.

"Ah, Lord Veryan." Lord Cheveley raised an eyeglass and through it surveyed his guest thoughtfully. "Have you come for your property? Well, well, I don't blame you. No, no, my dear, you run along. As a matter of fact I can see her ladyship waving at me which means something's up. Enjoy yourselves." He smiled benignly at them and moved away.

"You certainly seem to be enjoying yourself," muttered Lord Veryan after a moment.

"Oh yes!" she agreed brightly. "Mr. Waterhouse is very entertaining, you know, and as for Lord Cheveley, why he is quite droll! Do you not think so?"

"No, I don't!" he replied with suppressed violence. "And if you marked me you would not either! What do you mean by flaunting these men under my nose?"

She opened her eyes wide. "*Flaunting*, my lord? Upon my word, I do not understand you! Surely I am allowed to converse with your friends at an occasion like this?"

His eyes blazed at her. "Ay, ay, my friends! That's an easy one, that is! Call them my friends and then you can do what you like!"

"Christopher, you are attracting attention."

"Damn!" Lord Veryan wheeled round, and caught the eyes of his cousin, Sir Edward Carradale, across the room. Catching Katharine's arm, he bore her onto the floor, and, encircling her waist with his arm, joined in with the other waltzers.

"When I escort you to a ball, I expect at least a little attention from you!" he hissed above her.

Katharine fixed her gaze above his shoulder. "I cannot imagine what you are talking about. From what I saw, you did not appear to be missing me very much. In fact, you seemed vastly *epris*."

Lord Veryan gave her a quick glance. "Oh yes? And what do you mean by that?"

"I would have thought you could guess," she retorted immediately. "In fact, it makes me quite want to laugh when I think of what you said to me about calling them your friends and then doing what I like! You, I notice, do not hesitate to claim relations with Elizabeth!" Katharine felt his arm stiffen, and knew she had scored a hit.

"It is only natural that I should be pleasant to your brother's wife," he responded stiffly.

"Oh, ay, pleasant, but I did not know that included a tête a tête in the library!"

There was no answer. Katharine, risking a glance upwards, saw her husband tight-lipped and grim above her, and felt a small wave of satisfaction. He knew, now.

The dance was concluded in silence. Lord Veryan conducted his wife to the edge of the floor, bowed formally to her, and walked away. Katharine watched apprehensively as he threaded his way through the crowds towards his host, and stood talking with him for a short time. Then he bowed slightly, and in a moment had left the ball.

Katharine felt suddenly desolate. The room was filled with laughing, talking people, most of them she knew, but she nevertheless felt as though her one support had been removed. Then from across the room she saw Elizabeth, and determined to show no sign of the turmoil within.

And so the evening proceeded. Lord Cheveley approached Lady Veryan and said he was sorry her husband's business had called him away, and that had it not obviously been very important, would have been loth to let him go. He promised her his carriage whenever she should wish to leave, and said he hoped she did not mind remaining on behind her husband. Katharine smiled and said what she could, but could not help wondering just what the Marquis had said to so excuse himself.

The dancing recommenced, and Katharine found herself with no shortage of partners. Towards one o'clock, however, a message was brought to her through one of the flunkeys that Lord Veryan had returned and would await her in the library. According to the servant, said the man, Lord Veryan was particularly anxious to see her alone. Accordingly, he preceded her from the ball room, along a wide passage, and ushered her into a dimly-lit room.

Katharine was not surprised to be so summoned, nor did she find it hard to account for the privacy of the interview. Lord Veryan either wished to see her to argue with her, or to apologise, and in both these cases an audience would be decidedly *de trop*. Consequently she was quite unalarmed as she walked into the unfamiliar, book-lined room, and heard the servant snap the door shut behind her.

At first she thought it was quite empty. A branch of candles stood on the desk in the centre of the room, shedding a very inadequate light into the corners of the library. The room was heavy with shadow. She stepped further into the room and was about to turn round when a hand, firm and strong, pressed itself across her mouth and an arm wound round her neck.

She knew at once what was happening, and could have screamed with vexation that she should be so caught, when the matter had been under lively discussion only that evening. She sighed beneath the hand.

A soft chuckle came from behind her. "So," hissed a voice above her, "you know what I want, Lady Veryan, do you not! Keep very still and it will be over in a moment." The voice was sibilant, and, had Katharine not known by the strength of the arm that held her that it was a man, the voice would have told her nothing. The arm about her neck was removed, and she felt fingers at the nape of her neck. With one hand the man was pulling at the clasp of her necklace, but the fastening was stiff and would not move. With a soft oath the man above her bent over her head and whispered softly: "If you love your life, Lady Veryan, keep silence!" She nodded, and he removed his hand from her mouth. Katharine breathed deeply. The relief was incredible.

The thief was still struggling with the necklace, and began unwittingly to put pressure on Katharine's throat by pulling it from behind. "Sir," she whispered, with difficulty, "I am perfectly willing to let you have my necklace, but I had much rather you did not take my head with it!"

The fingers relaxed, and the chuckle sounded again. It was both familiar and infectious.

"I know you, don't I?" she said suddenly, and felt the fingers stiffen on her neck. "Oh, don't worry, I've no desire to become a liability! I don't mean I have recognised you, just that if I could see you, I would."

She sensed his smile as he said softly: "The necklace, my lady?"

Accordingly, Katharine raised one hand to the clasp, and, after a short struggle, had released it. She felt it caught and removed at once.

"And now, my lady, do not turn round, if you please." She heard him move away, and, in a moment, the door open and close. Of a sudden her legs felt weak and her head dizzy, and she sank gratefully onto a nearby leather-backed chair. Her necklace was gone, her beautiful necklace. Well, she thought practically, it was probably her own fault for being so taken-in by such a simple ruse. She sighed, and began considering the other extraordinary factor of the affair — the fact that she quite certainly was acquainted with the thief. She tried to run through the ranks of her friends, but her brain was functioning slowly, and she soon gave up the attempt. It did occur to her, however, that whoever it was had been party to her argument with her husband, and was therefore in all likelihood a guest at the ball. She realised too with a start that by sitting there in the semi-dark like an idiot when she should be raising the alarm she was considerably lessening her chances of recovering the precious heirloom. She stood up resolutely, therefore, and although her legs still felt ridiculously weak, she moved with determination to the door and succeeded in pulling it open. The passage was deserted. Steadying herself occasionally with a hand on the wall, she proceeded towards the glow of light that emanated from the ball room. Before reaching the crowd, however, she encountered a footman, and thankfully submitted to his support. He heard her story in growing concern — he was the very footman who had conveyed the message — and beckoned to another servant to fetch the master at once. Having seen Lady Veryan safely to a chair, he hurried down the stairs with the express purpose, he said, of summoning the Watch.

The story of Katharine's loss seemed to strike terror into the hearts of the ladies. Two had a fit of the vapours and a third, succumbing to mild hysterics, had to be carried bodily from the dance floor to the privacy of an adjoining room. Lord Cheveley was really vastly put out, and, to her amusement,

Katharine found herself assuring him that it was really no fault of his but her own entirely, since she had been so gullible as to fall for the trap.

Lord Cheveley shook his head. "That is kind of you, my dear, most kind, but the theft occurred in my house, and I am therefore responsible. Besides, it was one of my own footmen who conducted you into the trap. I shall quite understand if the Marquis demands restitution."

Katharine, thinking that her husband was far too easy-going for such a thing even to occur to him, ventured to say that she thought it unlikely.

"All the same," said Lord Cheveley wretchedly, "it is a bad business, bad indeed, that a villain should walk unmarked into our very midst!"

Katharine hesitated, and then said: "As to that I have my own theory. However, I shall not bore you with it now. I suppose I shall be obliged to answer innumerable questions?"

This remark seemed to bring Lord

Cheveley to his senses. "My dear Lady Veryan, you have had too much of a shock to undergo such a thing tonight! I shall escort you home myself, and the officers may call on you in the morning."

"Well," said Katharine doubtfully, "if you think that is advisable. They may not like it if I'm not here, you know."

"They will not be able to help it," sighed a voice behind her. "My lord, you are needed here," said Mr. Waterhouse. "I shall conduct her ladyship home with the greatest of pleasure."

There followed a slight, formal altercation between the two gentlemen which resulted, a few minutes later, in Katharine's wrap being placed about her shoulders, and her being conducted down the stairs and away by Mr. George Waterhouse.

7

WHEN the Marquis left Cheveley House his primary desire was to be alone. He had much to think about and felt unable to give his concerns the concentration they deserved whilst whirling round the floor to some waltz melody. He had had little compunction in leaving Katharine there, even though he had been acting as her escort. There were plenty of men willing to act for him, and if any of these failed, there was always Robert Sherreden, her brother. The fact that Katharine might not seek a ride home in the same carriage with her hated sister-in-law did not occur to him. He thought it an ideal solution. Almost instinctively he crossed over Mount Street and turned North along South Audley Street towards Grosvenor Square before realising what he was doing and deciding he did not want to go home at all. The possibility that Katharine might leave the ball after him could not but occur. He turned along Adam's Row, therefore, and, a few minutes later, found himself in Bond Street. From then on he wandered aimlessly, but away from fashionable London into the maze of streets around Soho.

The night was by no means warm. The sky was clear and dotted with stars, and a haze about the moon gave warning of a heavy frost. Beyond turning up the collar of his cloak Lord Veryan paid little attention to the chill that seeped into his bones, merely striding down narrow, unlit streets. As far as he could see, his life was in a complete mess. Elizabeth was beautiful, but he did not want her, and wished whole-heartedly that she would take herself off to plague some other hapless soul. If only he had not been so foolish with Katharine that afternoon then the argument would never have occurred.

But now Katharine was angry. She had shown that in very action that evening, and the Marquis began to wonder if he would ever succeed in winning her affections. At one point he had not been unhopeful. Of late Katharine had shown marked thawing of the chill towards him. Now, of course, that was all gone. Naturally she was angry with him. Who would not be at the thought of one's husband entertaining his mistress in the library. But then Katharine, too, had behaved badly, positively encouraging Waterhouse to dangle after her in that dreadful way.

He sighed. It was useless, of course, to defend himself. He was fond of Katharine, he had to admit it, and disliked having to hurt her. Stopping for a moment, he wondered whether he should go back and apologise, then, as visions of his wife in strong hysterics assailed him he hastily banished the idea, resolving not to encounter her until she could be counted on to receive him with chilling civility. He walked on, deeply despondent, hardly noticing where his steps were taking him.

After a while he stopped again and looked about him. He was in an area of London completely unknown to him, and he realized that, if he did not turn back, he would find himself hopelessly lost. He did turn, and began retracing his steps, but soon his thoughts drew him again and he began wandering as aimlessly as before.

It occurred to him to wonder now just how much of the argument Sir Edward Carradale had seen and deduced. The thought that it might be all reported to his grandfather was disturbing, and he began to regret showing his discontent so blatantly. He wondered, for the hundredth time, how much credit his Grace gave to Sir Edward's tales, and thought that, although it was probably not much, it was more than likely that he accepted the hard core as fact. The possibility that the Duke's favours might be withdrawn was too dreadful to contemplate, and the young Marquis put it resolutely from his mind.

As far as he could judge, he was now nearly back to the area of London that was familiar to him. The street he was in now, however, was narrower than most, and stretched away into darkness ahead. He knew it was late, probably after midnight, and it occurred to him now to worry about the chance of meeting with a party of mohocks. Some movement in the shadows ahead of him caused a little stir in his stomach, and he found himself grasping his slim cane more tightly and wishing it were still fashionable to wear swords. He moved into the shadows of the buildings on his left, and proceeded cautiously. He was vastly disconcerted by a wall springing up almost in front of him, and discovered after a moment that the road narrowed sharply and proceeded through an arch beneath a row of buildings. He stretched out a hand to the wall, and, following it along, gained the edge of the street again. Convinced though he was that there was someone near, it was nevertheless with a sharp jolt that he heard the scuffle of a boot on the pavement and caught part of a whispered conversation. Grasping his cane firmly by the silver top, he gained the corner of the arch and peered round.

Two men were there, and, he was relieved to discover, were apparently unaware of his presence. He was about to creep away when the conversation again floated in his direction and he found himself rivetted. Pressing himself against the wall he strained his ears to pick up the words, which all at once grew a little louder.

"Now see here," said the voice, twanging slightly of the cockney, "five hundred you promised me, and five hundred is what I want. I've risked my reputation for you, and more than once! Why should this job be so different from the last?"

His companion's reply was so soft that Lord Veryan could not hear it.

"I daresay," responded the other at his former pitch. "But how much do *you* get, that's what I want to know. Those rubies were very fine, you know, even split up as they must be by now. I think I'm within my rights to demand a little more!"

Lord Veryan's eyes widened in the darkness as he tried to catch a glimpse of the pair. But the passage was almost completely dark, the light thrown by a swinging lantern at the far end of the passage merely casting the couple into further obscurity.

"Three times I've come into the open for you, friend, and it isn't enough to say you've got no buyer. I could turn King's Evidence, you know, and land you in the dock!"

At last the other man seemed roused. Words came floating to Lord Veryan — 'grateful', 'penniless', 'emeralds'. He seemed to be trying to reason with the other man, but unsuccessfully. The cockney, the broader of the two, gave a harsh laugh, and began to move away.

Before Lord Veryan realised what was happening there was an explosion, and the man halted in his tracks. He stood motionless for a moment, silhouetted against the light from the lantern, then his legs folded beneath him and he crumpled onto the pavement. Lord Veryan gasped and grew incautious. The other man had approached the body and was now bending over it, but the sound Lord Veryan had made clearly reached him. He stood up, and the Marquis pressed himself hard against the wall. Footsteps sounded rapidly, and in a second a hand had pulled him into the moonlight. In silence the two men looked at each other then the murderer tossed the weapon in the direction of the body, gave a hollow laugh, and ran off down the street.

It took Lord Veryan a moment to gather his wits. He stared after Mr. Waterhouse, and then realized he should do something about the man on the pavement, in case he was yet alive. He approached him carefully, therefore, eyeing the pistol that lay nearby. The fellow was clearly dead, but as the Marquis felt in his pocket for some identification a man appeared at the end of the passage, a lantern held high in one hand.

"'Ere! What'r' you doing?"

Lord Veryan glanced up, and blinked in the light of the lantern held full in his face. Panic seized him. He knew how it would look to the fellow, and in a second was up and running down the street, leaving his hat and cane beside the body. For a few yards the officer of the Watch gave chase, but he was round and heavy and the Marquis soon outstripped him. He hesitated a moment, then with a grunt returned to the dead man.

Even as he ran Lord Veryan realized what a fool he had been. He had only to tell the fellow what and whom he had seen for it all to be cleared up, but somehow, since he had seen Mr. Waterhouse's face, he felt nothing was so simple any more. He knew the fellow to be cunning and clever, and, when caught, to be a decidedly slippery customer. No doubt he would adequately explain away his presence in that part of London while he, for the moment, was singularly confused.

After a while he realized there was no pursuit, and turned once more in a westerly direction. Walking briskly now, he soon found himself in Piccadilly. From there it was only a short distance to Duke Street. He had already decided not to go home that night, and, if only he were in, he knew he could command Mr. Malling's couch for the night. He approached his friend's lodgings in time to see Mr. Malling himself walking up from the opposite direction.

"Hello, Ver! What are you doing here?"

"Lend me your couch, Freddie, there's a good fellow."

"Of course, Ver, of course! What's happened, though? Where's Lady Ver?"

"Let me in, Freddie, and I'll tell you it all."

At last Mr. Malling seemed to take in his friend's hatless and dishevelled condition, and, beyond giving him a sharp stare, opened the door without more ado.

"Have some brandy, Ver," he said, as they gained his chambers. "You need it."

"Yes," agreed his lordship simply. "I've just seen a man murdered, Freddie."

Mr. Malling tipped the bottle rather recklessly, but beyond that gave no sign of the astonishment he felt. Silently he handed the glass to the Marquis, and saw him settled in a chair. Lord Veryan sighed, and took a sip of brandy.

"I argued with Katharine, stupid really, about Elizabeth. Anyway, I left the ball."

"Yes, I saw you go."

"You didn't see who escorted her home, by any chance?"

Mr. Malling shook his ginger head.

"Sorry, old chap I didn't stay. Left shortly after you with Bart."

"Oh. Well, I expect she got home alright. Sherreden was there, you know. He'd take her."

Mr. Malling raised a brow, but said nothing.

"I walked," continued the Marquis. "I just wanted to think, you understand. Anyway, I saw two men, arguing. And you'll never believe this, Freddie, but it was about those robberies. You know, the jewel robberies. Well, one of them seemed to be demanding more money which the other man did not like. Then the first man said he'd turn King's Evidence, and the second man shot him in the back with a pistol." He stared deep into the brandy in the glass.

Mr. Malling looked horrified. "Good God, Ver, this is dreadful! I suppose he ran off, this other fellow. Did you get a look at him?"

Lord Veryan glanced up, and laughed. "It was George."

Now Mr. Malling was speechless.

His mouth was open slightly and his blue eyes stared. "Not *George?* Waterhouse?"

"Waterhouse."

"Good God." Mr. Malling seemed astounded. "George a *murderer?* A thief too? Good God, the impudence of it! But look here, Ver, are you sure?"

"Oh yes, absolutely. He saw me, you know. It was George."

"And I suppose he knew you recognised him."

"Of course. He laughed, and ran off."

Mr. Malling looked thoughtful. "You know, Ver, this could be an awkward business. If George knows you saw, he could cut up pretty rough. After all, it's his neck on the block now. I wonder why he did it?"

"Money, I suppose. He plays deep, Freddie, deeper than any of us. Shouldn't be surprised if he were badly dipped. They say old Waterhouse ran through a half million in a year.

Couldn't credit it myself, but that's what they say."

Mr. Malling whistled. "I say, Ver, this could be nasty for you. Clever fellow, George. Shouldn't be surprised if he cut up rough. You know, I think it was wise not going to Clayre House tonight. Might be looking for you."

Lord Veryan looked up thoughtfully. "Damn," he said softly. "I could have done without this, Freddie. Do you think he'll try to kill me?"

Mr. Malling shrugged. "I can't say for sure, of course, but think of it, Ver, he's desperate! Look here, I think you ought to get out of town for a few days, just until this dies down. I'll tip the wink to the Runners about George, and let you know when it's safe to come back."

"Dash it, Freddie, I don't want to run away! I'd rather face him."

"Of course you would, Ver," said Mr. Malling soothingly. "But look here, I'd be surprised if it turned out like that. Have one over the top, fall under a

169

carriage, that sort of thing."

Lord Veryan looked struck.

"Lie low, Ver, take her ladyship out of town as I said."

The Marquis stared at the brandy glass cupped in his hands and said nothing for several minutes. "Listen, Freddie. I've a mind to do as you say, but I want your help. I saw George, what I know could be important. And dash it all, I've no mind to run off like a coward! So I want you to put me up. No, wait. I'll tell them all, Katty too, that I'm going out of town, and let them think what they like. But I want George, and I don't want him slipping away because they can't find anything to prove he did it. He's served me a back-handed turn more than once. Keep me here, Freddie, for a week or two, and let me see what happens."

Mr. Malling hesitated. "I'd like to, Ver, truly I would, but where would you sleep? There's only the couch, you know, and how would I explain it to my man, and to Mrs. Wilson downstairs?"

"Dash it, Freddie, we'll think of something."

"Look here, Ver, it wouldn't work. I'm sorry, but it wouldn't. Besides, George would be certain to come here first. Difficult fellow to resist, is George."

For a moment Lord Veryan looked daunted, then he grinned suddenly. "Tell you what, Freddie, I'll stay here tonight, then in the morning your man can get a room somewhere out of the way. How about that?"

Mr. Malling breathed a sigh of relief. The prospect of a permanent guest had not cheered him. "Certainly, Ver. If I might say so, I think that's a much better idea. You never know what I might let slip."

Lord Veryan looked struck. "No, by God! Thank you, Freddie, you're a great help. I'll tell her la'ship in the morning that I'm leaving town. I hope she understands."

Katharine's temper when she descended to breakfast the next morning and discovered her spouse had not returned all night was not happy. Of course, he was not to know that her necklace would be stolen when he left, but surely the news would have reached him by morning. She sighed, and wondered where he had spent the night. She herself had not slept well. The loss of her necklace and the fact that she knew the thief kept her awake equally, and it was nearly five o'clock when she finally drifted into uneasy slumber. And now Christopher was not even there to scold her for being so careless. She could not help wondering if Elizabeth knew where he was, and toyed with the idea of going to Grosvenor Street to see her. Pride prevented her, but she did wonder if she should make a point of being out when her husband finally appeared. In the event she was in her dressing room, and as her husband strode in with barely a knock she had no time to pretend she was either out or indisposed. Instead she glared at him in the mirror and demanded what he meant by bursting into the room in that way.

He sighed, and sank into a chair. "Oh, Katty, don't start arguing straight away. I've had the devil of a night."

It was an unfortunate thing to say and Katharine laughed bitterly. "I can imagine! But please don't bother me with it! I have enough troubles of my own!"

"I daresay you have, but I doubt if they are equal to mine! However, I do not wish to quarrel. I wanted to talk to you. The thing is, Katharine, I have to leave London for a spell."

The grey eyes glinted. "Indeed? And where, pray, are you thinking of going?"

"I thought I might go to Stannisburn and put it in order. Oh, dash it all, that's not the reason! I have to leave town."

"Do you? Do you? I wonder why, so suddenly, it is expedient for you to leave? Has your cousin Edward been speaking to you, or should I inquire the reason of Elizabeth?" The words had darted out before she could stop them, and she bit her lip, knowing it to have been a mistake to come so early to the point.

Lord Veryan stood up now, his face pale and drawn. "Why I am leaving has nothing to do with Elizabeth. It is because — "

"I don't want to know! You were content last night to leave me at Lady Cheveley's without a word or explanation. You may do the same now."

Lord Veryan regarded her gravely for a moment. Then he made a gesture of despair, bowed stiffly, and left the room. He crossed immediately to his own room where he ordered his startled valet to pack a couple of shirts and cravats in a bag.

"I am leaving town for a few weeks,"

he said shortly. "I shall not need you."

If the valet had been surprised at his master's sudden journey he was horrified that the young man was proposing to go quite unattended.

"I hope, my lord," he said woodenly, "that you are not dissatisfied with my work?"

Lord Veryan glanced up and gave a short laugh. "Don't talk rubbish, man. I'll be back. Of course I'm satisfied. Now get on with your business."

When Lord Veryan got back to Duke Street he found Mr. Malling just returned from his Club, having faithfully spread the word of the Marquis's departure from town. He was also the bearer of what were, for Lord Veryan, ill-tidings.

"Seen Lady Ver, have you? I suppose she's told you, then. Sad business."

"Just what, Freddie," demanded the Marquis, "are you talking about?"

Mr. Malling looked at his friend through narrowed lids. "She didn't tell you? Well, now, how do you account for that?"

"If you tell me, I might know."

"George stole her emeralds," he answered simply. "Last night after you left."

Lord Veryan sat down suddenly. "Good God! She said nothing at all, Freddie! Nothing! Mind you, she was pretty cut up about my not coming home last night. Hardly surprising, I suppose, in the circumstances. Odd, though, that she didn't tell me. George again, then. Dash it, Freddie, he was making up to her last night, too! I'm dashed if I don't kill him for this!"

Mr. Malling, eyeing his friend in some alarm, made haste to calm his anger by providing him with a hurried glass of wine. Lord Veryan, finding a glass pushed into his hand, stared at it uncomprehendingly for a moment, then transferred his gaze to his host.

"What the devil's this for, man? Take it away, or drink it yourself!"

Since his guest seemed inclined to

empty the liquid on the floor unless relieved of the glass immediately, Mr. Malling seized it hurriedly and set it on the winetable.

"Did you see George?" demanded Lord Veryan after a moment.

Mr. Malling eyed him warily. "He was there," he responded at last. "Apparently he escorted her la'ship home last night."

Lord Veryan slammed his hand on the upholstered arm of the chair and raised a cloud of dust. "Damn his impudence! I ask you, Freddie, had you ever heard the like? I've a mind to call him out."

"Shouldn't do that, Ver, if I were you. Crack shot, you know."

Lord Veryan sank back into the chair he had hurriedly vacated. "You're right, Freddie," he conceded, "but damn it all, what can a fellow do about a villain like George? I can't just sit here while he gallivants all over London stealing jewels and murdering his henchmen!"

Mr. Malling looked thoughtful. "Thing is, Ver, George was asking after you. Asked me if I'd seen you, so I said what you told me, how you stayed here last night, and were going to Stannisburn in the morning."

"Hmm, asked, did he? Well, thank you, Freddie, I'm obliged. When will you go to Bow Street?"

"When you're safely out of the way, old fellow, not before. Slippery character, our George. Best to take care."

"When will that man of yours be back? I only hope he gets me something decent."

The room, to Lord Veryan's disgust, was in Kensington. What, he demanded, had possessed the fellow to choose such an out of the way place as Kensington? And when Ferbridge replied that his lordship had instructed him to find something genteel but not fashionable, Lord Veryan had testily responded that he had not expected to be taken so dashed literally. To Kensington, however, he was to go, and departed almost immediately in a hansom cab, Mr. Malling having first scoured Duke Street for lurking spies.

8

HER husband's departure left Lady Veryan feeling very low. She knew she should have told the Marquis about the theft of what was, after all, his property, but somehow the loss of the emeralds seemed insignificant. What, she wondered, could possibly be the reason for Lord Veryan's sudden departure? Surely not just this argument the night before? He could not be so foolish. All the same, she wished she had given him a chance to tell her, and now that he was gone she began to worry about just when he would return. A week or two, he had said, but Katharine knew her husband well enough to be aware that for him time was a flexible thing. Surely he would not be so brazen as to take Elizabeth to Stannisburn? But why else would he depart so suddenly? It was all too provoking.

So occupied was Katharine with her marital problems that she completely forgot that law officers would be coming that morning to question her. She was still upstairs where Lord Veryan had left her when the message was conveyed, and startled her into sudden activity.

She entered the drawing room to find it occupied by two solemn-looking individuals in sombre black. Of these, it turned out that one was to be her questioner, while the other, an insignificant little man with a worried look, was present to transcribe the conversation.

From the start Katharine found the interview slightly ridiculous. The Constable was a pompous individual with a large nose and receding hair, and seemed to think Lady Veryan had been remarkably careless.

"If I might be permitted, my lady," he began, seating himself at her invitation, "if you ladies of rank were more attentive, and paid greater care to your jewels, we would never be obliged to pursue inquiries of this nature. However, since the robbery has been perpetrated, we must do our best, mustn't we, to recover your property. I'm sure you will do all you can to assist us."

"Naturally," Lady Veryan replied, somewhat coolly. "However, I do think I ought to tell you that the thief was behind me all the time and spoke in a whisper, so I could identify neither his face nor his voice. The accomplice I did not see."

"Ah. Well, as far as the accomplice is concerned, my lady, we have, for once, obtained a fairly reliable statement from the lackey. In fact, I might go so far as to say we have certain hopes in that direction. However, I am not here to discuss *that*." He looked sternly at Lady Veryan. "Perhaps you could tell me, Lady Veryan, at what time you were summoned exactly."

"Well, I believe it was about one o'clock. Yes, it must have been, because I arrived back home about forty-five minutes later, at a quarter before two."

The smaller officer began writing furiously.

"I see." The questioner nodded thoughtfully. "And what exactly did the lackey say?"

"That my husband was waiting to see me in the library."

"Your husband had told the lackey himself?"

"No, of course not! The accomplice told him, although of course the lackey just referred to him as Lord Veryan's servant."

"Hmm. And what, do you suppose, made him believe it was Lord Veryan's servant?"

"I really have no idea. You must ask him that, though I would presume it was because that was what the man said."

"I see. Yes, that would seem to be the case. So, you went to the library, escorted, or unescorted?"

"The lackey took me, but did not enter the room."

"I see. And you saw no one at all in or near the room?"

"No one."

"Thank you. Now, once in the library what happened?"

"A man seized me from behind and tried to unfasten the necklace, but the clasp was stiff and he couldn't do it. He had one hand over my mouth and he had to take it away to unfasten the clasp."

"Did you cry out?"

"He made me promise not to."

"So he spoke to you."

"Yes, but as I said, it was in a whisper."

"I see. So he got the necklace undone at last."

"No. It was stiff. I had to undo it myself."

"Indeed! You unfastened your own necklace and handed it to the thief! Is that natural behaviour?"

Lady Veryan raised her brows. "Of course. I had no desire to be strangled, I can assure you."

The Constable eyed her thoughtfully while the scribe continued to scratch busily. "No doubt it is as you say. What then?"

"The thief left, and I sat down for a moment. Then I left the room and summoned help."

"Help?"

"A servant went for the Watch."

"Ah, yes, the Watch. Unfortunately there was no sign of the thief, who had escaped, no doubt, while you were sitting down for a moment."

Lady Veryan glared at him.

"Well, Lady Veryan, I am sure you have been a great help. Is there anything else you can think of?"

"Yes, one thing. Something about the thief, his laugh, was familiar to me. I felt I had met him somewhere. In fact, it seemed to me that the thief must have been a guest that evening since he knew my husband had gone."

"You say you *knew* the thief?"

"I said I felt that he was among my

acquaintances, yes, but I could not tell you who he was." The scratching of the quill became fevered.

"I see. Well, that is all, I think, Lady Veryan. Just one thing. Is your husband at home?"

Katharine hesitated, and felt her colour rising. "No, he left this morning for Stannisburn."

"Leaving you to bear your distress alone. Good day, Lady Veryan."

The departure of the law officers was a great relief to Katharine. She felt, extraordinary though it undoubtedly was, that the men suspected her of some knowledge she had not imparted, and this feeling remained with her throughout the day. It was illogical, as well she knew, for she had told them everything, including the fact that the thief was known to her, a piece of information that must surely help them considerably.

It was with an effort during the next few days that Katharine maintained her social programme. The fear that she would be obliged to cry off from various engagements through not having an escort proved groundless, Elizabeth for some reason being willing to send her carriage for Katharine. On the one occasion that Elizabeth had not been invited an excellent escort provided himself in the form of Mr. George Waterhouse, whom Katharine did not scruple to accept since, besides being such a close friend of her husband's, he had already proved himself to be a valuable companion. She was, moreover, a married lady, and as such it could hardly be unacceptable for her to be seen abroad with such a popular and presentable gentleman. After this first occasion Mr. Waterhouse pronounced himself available whenever she should desire his company, and Katharine found herself attending quite as many functions as ever. She hoped that Lord Veryan was receiving regular reports about her enjoyment. This was marked. Wherever she was, Katharine gave every sign of enjoying herself hugely, and if the laughing and smiling countenance very often concealed a heavy heart no indication of this was apparent.

"She certainly doesn't seem to be missing that flighty husband of hers," remarked Lady Peterman as she and her companion watched Katharine and Mr. Waterhouse together at a ball. "Mind you, I never thought it a suitable match. He's too unsettled for her. Pity. I quite like the girl myself."

Miss Scurby agreed, and the two continued to observe the couple. "They say he's at Stannisburn," ventured Miss Scurby after a moment. "There's no reason to disbelieve it, I suppose?"

"Oh no, none at all, as far as I know. Of course, no one's been to Stannisburn to *check*."

Miss Scurby shook her head sadly. "She seems to be consoling herself anyway," she said, as Mr. Waterhouse conducted his partner onto the floor. "Of course, I'm not surprised. He is not unattractive."

"Oh no! Quite obvious what is going on *there*."

The occasion was Lady Crawley's ball, and Katharine, attired in a gown returned only that day from the dressmaker, looked remarkably fine. She was growing accustomed to attending functions without her husband and had been quite enjoying herself when a young woman approached her with a smile.

"Lady Veryan!" exclaimed Miss Marshall, regarding Katharine out of coolly calculating blue eyes. "How delightful to see you here! Tell me, is the Marquis near? I am dying for a word with him."

Katharine smiled stiffly. "Lord Veryan is still at Stannisburn, Miss Marshall. I am sure he will be very sorry to have missed talking to you."

"At Stannisburn?" echoed Miss Marshall, opening her eyes wide. "But how can that be? I distinctly saw him walking this morning in Kensington when I was out with Mama!"

Katharine raised her brows. "You must be mistaken. Lord Veryan is not expected back for several days."

"Indeed I am not, I assure you! Mama was with me and will tell you precisely the same!"

"Forgive me, Miss Marshall, but it could not have been the Marquis. Someone like him, perhaps."

Miss Marshall eyed Katharine sternly for a moment and then said: "I am sure you may say what you like, but I know it was he," and walked away.

"What impudence!" thought Katharine, turning away. All the same she was puzzled. For Miss Marshall to be so certain, so convinced that it had been Lord Veryan, and in Kensington too, of all places, was really very strange. Could it possibly be that Christopher was in London after all? But he had said so plainly that he was going to Stannisburn! What possible reason could he have for lying to her?

It was obvious, of course, and

Katharine's eyes involuntarily rested on her sister-in-law across the room. He must be seeing Elizabeth, must have been seeing her all this time, all those days that Katharine had spent alone wondering just what he was doing in Hampshire without his valet. Her simplicity even made her laugh. But it was extraordinary, nevertheless, and, Katharine thought, very unlike her husband. He had not seemed the sort to hide himself away merely to facilitate the enjoyment of an illicit affair. But then the prospect of his having married her simply to be near Elizabeth had not occurred to her either at the time. Standing thus engrossed on the edge of the floor she failed to see Mr. Malling approaching her, and jumped when he laid a hand on her arm.

"Oh, Freddie! I am so sorry! Have you been her long?"

"No. Thought I'd come across. Had a letter from Lord Veryan today. It occurred to me you might like to know. Says he's doing well enough in Hampshire."

Lady Veryan's eyes blazed. "Indeed?" she replied, her voice deceptively calm. "Perhaps you'd care to tell me how he finds Kensington as well!"

Mr. Malling paled and took a step backwards. "Kensington? My dear Lady Ver, what are you talking about?"

She laughed. "Oh, Freddie, can you do no better? I'm sure you think you're protecting him, and I only hope he appreciates it, but he has been seen, you know, this morning, by Miss Marshall and her mother."

Mr. Marshall assumed an expression of astonishment. "Ver? In Kensington? Now I really had no idea! I wonder what he was doing there? Funny he didn't tell me."

"Yes, wasn't it, especially since you received that letter from him in Hampshire!"

Mr. Malling began to look flustered. "Indeed, Lady Veryan, I am as mystified as you are! I can only suppose he returned suddenly. Perhaps he had some business there," he suggested suddenly.

Katharine took pity on him. "Don't worry, Freddie, I'm not angry with you. I'm sure it does you credit to defend him like that. Just do one thing for me."

"Of course, Lady Veryan, anything," responded Mr. Malling at once, his face scarlet.

"You might tell him I know he's here. I'd be grateful." She smiled as on a child, and moved away. Mr. Malling, wondering just what he had allowed himself to be talked into, hesitated a moment, then went in search of his hostess and rapidly quitted the ball. He felt himself to be very badly done by. He had gone to the ball at Lord Veryan's express desire, purposefully to convey the news that his lordship was well. And now the Marquis had been fool enough not only to go out, but to get himself seen whilst doing so. He began to feel that rather too much was being expected of his friendship.

Katharine did not stay much longer either. She began to feel dissatisfied with the collection of people present, then with the dancing, then with entertainment in any form. Before very long this had transmuted itself into a great tiredness and a violent desire to be at home. No sooner had she conveyed her wishes in a weary undervoice to her escort than she found herself guided from the floor and heading for her hostess and in a moment was seated in the comfortably sprung carriage for the short journey home.

"How kind you are, Mr. Waterhouse, to bring me home so promptly! I hope I have not spoiled your own enjoyment."

"Naturally you have not, since it is wholly dependent on yours."

She opened her eyes at that, and thoughtfully contemplated him as he sat opposite her. But there was little of the lover in his expression, which was, indeed, mildly amused, and she relaxed back against the squabs.

"Lord Veryan is at Stannisburn, I hear," said Mr. Waterhouse casually, as the carriage turned into South Audley Street.

"Yes," Katharine responded with an effort. "He has some business there."

"I am going into Hampshire myself shortly. Perhaps I might call on him."

Katharine gave a short laugh. "Pray give him my regards, if you see him."

Mr. Waterhouse contemplated her gravely.

Katharine's exhaustion as she climbed into bed was extreme, and it was with infinite relief that she blew out the candle and closed her eyes. The morning seemed to arrive in a matter of minutes, and found her little refreshed. She had an appointment that morning with her dressmaker, but was tempted to delay it. Common sense prevailed, however, and she went, realizing that little would be gained by her sitting in the house, thinking.

She returned to find her presence awaited. The law officers, the same that had visited her before, were in the front parlour, and had remained there, according to the butler, for an hour already. Katharine, thinking that such persons should not be kept kicking their heels for longer than was necessary, took off her hat in the hall, and proceeded straight into the front parlour.

The taller of the two was by the window, and when she encountered his gaze Katharine knew he was not in a conciliatory mood. The smaller man was studiously contemplating the carpet.

"Good day, gentlemen, I hope you have not been waiting long. Would you care for some refreshment?"

"Your butler has already offered us refreshment, my lady, which, I might add, we did not hesitate to decline. It is not our policy to drink liquor during an investigation."

Katharine said "Oh", and sat down.

The Constable, after regarding her gravely for a moment, moved back to the window and stood staring into the street.

"Lady Veryan," he began, without turning to her, "where is your husband?"

She raised her brows. "In Hampshire. I believe I told you."

"You told us he was in Hampshire, my lady, certainly. However, I feel obliged to inform you that he is *not*, nor are the staff in any expectation of his arrival." He turned now and eyed her keenly. Katharine remained silent. "I feel I ought to tell you, Lady Veryan, that the situation is extremely grave. *Extremely*." He waited for some response, which, being unforthcoming, he was obliged to provide himself. "We are shocked, of course, at such a thing, but it is by no means the first time such an event has occurred." He noticed with satisfaction that Lady Veryan was looking bewildered.

"Please explain. I have no idea what you are speaking of."

"Ah. Have you not? It is simple, my lady. The evidence against your husband, the Marquis of Veryan, is very strong. We believe him to be responsible for the recent society thefts."

Katharine stared at him a moment, then gave a laugh of sheer amusement. "Christopher? Why, how can you be so absurd? Apart from anything else, have you forgotten already that my jewels were among those stolen?"

The officer looked at her sternly. "Indeed not, Lady Veryan, indeed not! It was that very occurrence that made us consider his lordship with any seriousness."

Katharine looked at him in astonishment. "But this is ridiculous! Why should Christopher steal his own property? Upon my word, you would do better to look to some of the guests at Lady Cheveley's ball."

"I am sure that is what you think, my lady. However, we are now convinced that your husband is the thief. He has been very cunning, of course; stealing your jewels was designed to put us off his track, and might have succeeded, but for the very valuable evidence of a member of the public."

Katharine felt a sudden flutter in her chest. "Indeed?" she responded, her voice sounding very thin and nervous.

The officer returned to his contemplation of the street. "We have discovered the identity of the accomplice."

Katharine's heart lifted. "You have? Then surely he may be of some help?"

"I daresay he might, my lady, had he not been shot through the heart!" He hesitated a moment to observe the effect of his statement, and, seeing Katharine pale and horrified, he continued complacently. "I am sorry to have to tell you that your husband was seen to shoot the fellow in the back. The gentleman was certain it was Lord Veryan because, it seems, he is intimately acquainted with his lordship. Besides this, the Officer of the Watch who discovered the body saw a man bending over it, and will, I am certain, identify this man as your husband." He paused, and stood swaying on his heels by the window.

For Katharine, the situation was rapidly taking on the appearance of a nightmare. It was so terrible that it refused to penetrate her understanding, and she stared at the officer with bewilderment and horror blatant on her face.

"Trotter, bring out the articles, if you please." The small officer, thus addressed by his superior, sprang to his feet, and tenderly placed a silver-topped cane and a dusty beaver on the table before Lady Veryan. "Perhaps you could tell me, Lady Veryan," continued her persecutor gleefully, "whether you recognise these articles which are now before you as your husband's."

Katharine stood up, and ran one unsteady hand along the ebony cane. "They are like my husband's, yes, but I cannot be sure. There is nothing extraordinary about the design of either."

"As you say, Lady Veryan, there is not. However, I am sure you will find, when I tell you that these were discovered in the vicinity of the aforementioned body, that the case against your husband is severe. Also, Lady Veryan, there is the matter of your own evidence. You will remember saying, of course, that you recognised the gentleman."

Katharine jumped, and stared up at the officer, standing now in a threatening position over her. She gave an unsteady laugh. "Surely, surely you cannot take that to mean I knew it was my husband who took the jewels, even supposing it was he, which I take leave to doubt!"

"I will do you the justice of saying that you might not have known it was your husband, although I have my own opinion on that subject also. But I accept for the moment what you said, that the laugh was familiar to you."

"But this is altogether preposterous! Do you think if my husband stood behind me I would not know it?"

The officer shrugged and looked at her significantly. "Then there is the matter of your handing the jewels to the thief. Is that not extraordinary behaviour?"

"But I explained that! He was almost pulling my head off!"

The officer sighed. "Very well, my lady. But consider, if you will, the overwhelming weight of the other evidence. The lackey who told you *Lord Veryan* wanted to see you. I have a witness to testify that your husband said at his club one day that he was on Lady Jefford's balcony on the same evening that the Winslow necklace was stolen, and on another occasion that his lordship greatly admired the workings of the thief. There is his hat and his cane on the table before you. But, besides all this, I have one more thing to put to you. It was well known by his friends and associates that Lord Veryan had problems with his finances; also, if you will forgive me, Lady Veryan, that you were practically dowerless when he married you. Perhaps you would care to tell me, therefore, how you manage to live in this fashion?"

Katharine was on her feet, her eyes blazing. "Sir, you are insulting! Lord Veryan is heir to the Duke of Clayre. It is only fitting that he should live elegantly. As for your other suggestions, I find them all preposterous! That the Marquis of Veryan should stoop to such a thing is unthinkable! I am sorry if you are deprived of a quick solution, but you must look elsewhere for your murderer!"

The officer eyed her stonily. "I think, my lady, that your own part in this affair had escaped your notice. I take leave to tell you, Lady Veryan, that your actions are to be observed. We do not give up easily. Trotter, the articles." Trotter, who had transcribed — nothing during the entire interview, promptly gathered up the cane and hat and the two, without waiting for the butler, left Katharine alone.

Feeling dazed, Katharine sank back into the chair. There was a weakness in her knees and her head, usually so clear and reliable, was full of confused and conflicting thoughts. For a moment she thought she would faint, something she had not done in her life, and hurriedly dropped her head onto her knees. She remained thus for several minutes, until the servant entered with the news that the two gentlemen had left, but would be calling again in a few days. The knowledge that she would have it all to bear again proved too much. Her head grew light, stars danced before her eyes, and she fainted back onto the chair.

9

LORD VERYAN sighed and flicked over the page despondently. He had not known it would be so boring shut away in Kensington or he almost certainly would not have agreed to it. The books provided for him by Mr. Malling were worse than useless, consisting mostly of the novels his sister enjoyed. Lord Veryan had read two with moderate enjoyment, but, on embarking upon a third, he had discovered it to contain the same formula as the other two, and had thrown it away in disgust. He had had enough of ghosts and screams, black veils and worm-eaten bodies that were not really worm-eaten at all. So he had asked for history, and at his first attempt Mr. Malling had done rather well, producing something of Mr. Robertson's that had enabled him to while away several dull hours. But now it was really becoming too much to bear. Mr. Malling had nothing to report. Mr. Waterhouse was as much in evidence as ever, and although Mr. Malling had faithfully given in the information at Bow Street, little, or nothing, had come of it. The Marquis was in despair. He saw no end to his confinement, and began to wonder if he had been wise to pursue such a negative course. And then only yesterday morning he had taken a chance; had gone for a stroll in one of the less fashionable of Kensington's streets, and had had the misfortune to be passed and waved at by Mrs. Marshall and her gossiping daughter. It was all too provoking. He began to wonder whether anything would be gained by shutting himself away and was toying with the idea of facing Mr. Waterhouse at the end of a sword when Mr. Malling appeared at the door. Lord Veryan eyed him doubtfully, then tossed aside his book with a sigh.

"Well, Freddie, I hope you've brought me some better news."

Mr. Malling reddened a little as he said: "Nothing's happened with George, I'm afraid, but I went to the ball as you asked."

Lord Veryan's eyes brightened slightly, and he regarded his friend hopefully. "Did you see her, Freddie? Is she well?"

Mr. Malling answered cautiously. "She looked well, yes, but I'm afraid she knows, Ver. Miss Marshall saw you, you know, and she told Lady Ver."

"The Devil take the woman," exclaimed Lord Veryan, slamming his hand on the table. "Was there ever anything like my luck, Freddie?" He pondered a moment, then cursed afresh. "Now I suppose Katharine thinks I've been seeing Elizabeth all this time! Really, Freddie, this is getting too much for a fellow to bear!"

"She told me to tell you she knows you're here," said Mr. Malling, red with embarrassment. He added, after a moment: "She wasn't very pleased, Ver."

"I'm not surprised," responded the Marquis with feeling. "Look here, Freddie, unless you give me a reason, I shan't stay here. I've gained nothing at all by shutting myself away in this cursed stupid fashion!"

Mr. Malling began to look harassed. "I know it's boring, Ver, but do be sensible. I've a nasty feeling George has some trick up his sleeve. There were a couple of fellows asking some dashed odd questions at the club the other day."

Lord Veryan eyed him suspiciously. "What sort of questions?"

"About how you pass your leisure hours, and where you got the blunt to live as you do."

"Good God!" The Marquis was clearly horrified. "What the devil has the fellow been saying, Freddie? I'm damned if I don't get this settled once and for all!" He made a grab for his coat but Mr. Malling, now seriously alarmed, positioned himself between his friend and the door.

"Steady on, old fellow, nothing to fire up about. Remember he's a crack shot!"

"You forget, I've seen just how George handles a pistol! I know he's likely to put a bullet through me, but how can I let him get away with this? He's going to get me hung for his murder!"

"Yes," responded Mr. Malling mildly, "I rather think he has that in mind. Slippery fellow, our George. But listen, Ver, you can't go off with a loaded pistol to a fellow like George! He'd have you clapped up, sure as check!"

Lord Veryan eyed him fulminatingly, but gradually the rage subsided. "But dash it, Freddie, how can I sit here and let him do what he likes? It just isn't possible!"

Mr. Malling sighed. The situation was testing all his diplomacy. "Nevertheless, Ver, it's what you must do. If you tackle George now it will look very bad indeed!"

The Marquis cast his friend a despairing look. "If I sit here it will get worse! And besides all that, there's my wife thinking I'm having an affair with her sister-in-law! Upon my word, Freddie, it's outside of enough."

"To be sure it is, but truly, Ver, I fail to see what you can do. No sense in getting hanged, old fellow."

"No, but there is something I can do, and by God I shall, and you're going to help me!"

Mr. Malling raised a protesting hand. "Hey, steady on, I don't want to get shot either!"

"Don't be a fool, Freddie. You can go downstairs and find me a cab. I'm going to Sherreden's."

Mr. Malling's rosy countenance took on a haggard expression. "Lud, Ver, what are you at now? What on earth can be gained by going there?"

"The truth, at least as far as she is concerned. She can tell Katharine there is nothing between us, and by God she will. That she owes me, at least."

"Now, Ver, I'm not so sure you should do this. It won't do for you to be seen, you know, and riding about in a hackney ain't my idea of secrecy."

"Which is why I need your help. Summon me a hackney, there's a good fellow. I shall want you to make sure nobody sees me."

Mr. Malling's protestations went unheeded. In this Lord Veryan was resolved, and within a few minutes Mr. Malling had capitulated and been sent out into the street. It was a while before he returned, and the Marquis was wondering whether he had taken to his heels when the gentleman reappeared, a carriage having been engaged and waiting at the door.

"Now you go down ahead of me, Freddie, and make sure Miss Marshall is not waiting outside to wave at me."

Mr. Malling sighed, but descended before his friend, thankful only that he had prevented the young man from mere precipitate action. His manner when he gained the street was calculated to draw the attention of the most unsuspicious of observers but the Marquis, beyond exciting the stare of the driver, climbed into the hackney unmarked. In a moment they were clattering down the street, and Mr. Malling, whose nerves had been fully stretched, was able at last to relax. He glanced round at his friend.

The Marquis of Veryan was seated on the floor, regardless alike of protocol and his coat, which was making an excellent job of sweeping up the dust. Mr. Malling, knowing remonstrance to be useless, merely rolled his eyes heavenwards, and fixed his gaze firmly on the trees of Hyde Park.

"What if her la'ship ain't in?" he said suddenly, persuading himself to look at the figure on the floor.

"If she's not in, I shall have to wait, Freddie, and so shall you."

"Yes, but dash it all, Ver, she may be

all day!" he expostulated weakly. Lord Veryan gave him a quelling glance.

After a little while the carriage was brought to a halt, and Mr. Malling looked cautiously out onto the tall house in Upper Grosvenor Street. His role, he discovered, was merely to remain in the carriage until Lord Veryan returned, a passive part that wrung a sigh of relief from that over-wrought gentleman. After carefully scanning the street, he beckoned Lord Veryan out, and after seeing him safely up the steps, returned to sit in the carriage.

Her ladyship was in, but on the point of setting out for a turn in the park. The news that his lordship was below made her raise her brows in surprise, and slowly draw off her lavender kid gloves. A few minutes later she appeared in the drawing room doorway, and stood regarding her visitor through thick, dark lashes.

"So, my lord, you are not in Hampshire after all!"

Lord Veryan grimaced at that, and unceremoniously pulled her into the room and shut the door. "Never mind that. The thing is, Lizzy, I want you to do something for me."

She opened her eyes wide. "Do you, now! What, I wonder, could *I* possibly do for you?"

He eyed her exasperatedly and started pacing the floor. "I want you to see Katharine and tell her the truth. Tell her there is nothing between us, and what there was was all over when I got married."

Lady Sherreden contemplated him thoughtfully. "I'm sure you have your reasons, Christopher, but why should you want me to tell such a lie?"

"Dash it, Lizzy," exclaimed his lordship impatiently, "it's no lie, as well you know! Anything we had was over months ago. It would be a simple thing for you to do."

"Doubtless, but I fail to see why I should."

"Look here, Lizzy, you know perfectly

214

well that you've done your best to make Katty jealous. For some reason it pleases you to make her unhappy, though why, I can't imagine. Why must you ruin our happiness, Lizzy? For some whim or other? It is not much I ask, and would mean a lot to both of us."

A light glinted in the blue eyes. "Would it, indeed? I don't know what makes you think I should want to help Katty. She's stuck up and prim, and fit for nothing but looking after other people's children. I wonder you don't see it, knowing her as you do."

"That's unfair, Elizabeth, you know it is. Katty may not be like you, but she has a great deal you lack. She's kind, for one thing."

"Ho, so it's kindness, is it? Well, let me tell you, Christopher, there's no kindness in love, and never will be. Katty's weak, I always knew it, which was why you chose me and not her in the first place. I would have made you a good wife, and now I'll make you a good mistress. But see Katharine I will not."

Lord Veryan gave a short laugh. "I have a wife, Elizabeth, and I certainly don't want a mistress! You owe me this, for making such trouble. I've a mind to see Sherreden."

It was her turn to laugh. "Do you really think he'd care? Besides, I would have thought you had other things to worry about apart from that silly wife of yours."

Lord Veryan had been pacing the floor, but he stopped at this and approached her with rapid steps. "What do you mean?"

She tittered. "Jewels is what I mean, Christopher, I'm surprised you didn't guess. Two law officers were here, asking me where you were. It seems they went to Stannisburn, but didn't find you. It's about a murder, or some such thing. They seemed to think I should know where you were, why, I can't imagine."

Lord Veryan ran a hand through his

already disordered locks. "So it is that, then! I should have guessed! I never thought even he would do such a thing! Look, Lizzy, if they've told you, they've told Katharine. You must see her now and set her mind at ease."

"About what, pray? I've no mind to lie, Christopher, and I shan't forget quickly how you looked at me in your library."

He cursed then, and ran a hand across his brow. Searching mechanically in his pocket he found his snuff box, and absently inhaled. "Look, Lizzy," he said, dropping the snuff box on the table, "you must help me, this is serious. I'm sure I need not tell you I had nothing to do with those thefts, but Katty might be worried. She's bound to be, in fact."

She regarded him with amusement. "I am desolated, Christopher", and laughed.

There came a soft knock. Lady Sherreden, after glancing at her harassed guest, moved to the door and opened it herself.

"Lady Veryan is below, my lady. Shall I send her up?"

Lady Sherreden's eyes lit up with mischief as she contemplated the butler. "Give me one minute, Horden, then ask her to step upstairs. I shall receive her here."

Lord Veryan, who had heard this exchange, looked horrified, and for a moment was quite speechless. "Elizabeth!" he ejaculated at last. "She cannot find me here! I must hide!"

"Yes," she agreed calmly, picking up his gloves from where he had dropped them. She opened a door into an adjoining room and Lord Veryan, his face white, passed through, collecting his gloves as he went. As he shut the door Lady Sherreden's eye fell on the snuff box, an enamelled piece with a distinctive design. For a moment she fingered it thoughtfully, then, with a little smile, set it back on the table.

Katharine was not a little confused.

She had walked the short distance to Upper Grosvenor Street in a state of indecision, and had almost resolved not to go in when the sight of Mr. Malling's harassed countenance gave her pause. He was clearly aghast to see her, and darted into a waiting carriage which at once moved off, only to stop again a few yards further down the road. Katharine's eyes narrowed, and she glanced up at her brother's house. Then on an impulse she ran up the steps and sharply pulled the bell. Now, as she waited anxiously in the hall, she felt her temper rising, and almost expected Elizabeth to be refused. She was not, however, and in a little while the butler returned and conducted her upstairs.

What she expected to find she was not sure, but when she entered the room it did not need the sight of his snuff box to inform her that her husband had been there. Elizabeth, smiling and smug, told her what she needed to know.

Just what had brought her to Upper Grosvenor Street she was not sure, a vague hope of discovering some explanation, perhaps, but now she was there she had no doubts. The grey eyes glinted as she contemplated her hated sister-in-law. "I should have guessed, I suppose," she said, ignoring Elizabeth's invitation to be seated, "but I had thought that even you could not be so brazen! How can you sit there, looking so smug?"

Elizabeth stood up, and faced her angry sister-in-law. "It is not I, Katharine, who makes you angry. Only your husband can offend you. If he really loved you there would be no need for anger. I would have no place in his life."

"I am sure what you say is correct, Elizabeth," Katharine replied with forced calmness. "I have a great deal to learn, it seems. Have the goodness, however, to inform my husband that he is in great danger from the Authorities. They suspect him of theft and murder.

I own, until now I had not thought him capable of it, but now I could believe anything."

Her words precipitated an unexpected reaction. Lord Veryan, listening in the next room, wrenched open the door and marched in to confront his wife.

"Katharine, none of this is true! I am no more a murderer than you are! You must believe me!"

"How can I, when I find you here, where, no doubt, you have been since you left me last week!"

"Indeed, Katharine, it is not so! Elizabeth, tell her!"

"I, Christopher? What should I tell?"

"Katharine! You must believe me! I don't want her!"

He had grasped her arms tightly, and now with an effort she wrenched herself free. "I don't know what to believe! Leave me alone!" So saying, she cast a fierce glance round the room, and swept herself out.

Mr. Malling's carriage was still waiting as Katharine ran down the steps, but she passed it without a glance. She had formed her resolve in the time it took to gain the front door, and meant to have no delay in executing it. The fact that her intended refuge was the home of her husband's grandfather was merely unfortunate. She meant to leave London, and had no choice. That he would receive her she had no doubt. A bond had been formed between them and the knowledge that she was sheltering from his heir would not, she was sure, affect his promise of help.

She made her way back to Grosvenor Square half-running and half-walking, frequently glancing over her shoulder to make sure no one followed. But the street was empty. Arriving back at Clayre House she could barely wait for the door to be opened, and agitatedly begged the butler, if her husband should come, to tell him she was not yet returned. She was halfway up the stairs before she recollected, and turned to the butler once more.

"Lowell, please could you see about the hiring of a chaise and four? I need it as soon as possible. I shall be going to Cheard for a while."

Lowell, registering no surprise, merely bowed, and set about delegating the work.

A hasty review of her wardrobe quickly informed Katharine that she could not, as she would have wished, take only those clothes her husband had not bought her. Her old gowns had long since been given away, and those items of underwear that remained were now quite distasteful to her. Sighing quietly, she selected half a dozen of her plainest gowns, and resolutely shut the door on Mme. Denise's more splendid creations. She would be obliged, too, to use the Marquis's money to convey her there, but a very little heart-searching persuaded her that this could not be wrong. She reflected grimly that he would not have had it at all had it not been for her.

Ellie was clearly surprised at the suddenness of the journey, but a visit to the Duke was, after all, unexceptional, and she set about packing the few gowns with no more than a raised eyebrow. She was not averse to a journey into Somersetshire, even though the season was at its height, for the attentions of the second footman were becoming marked, and Mr. Lowell had already signified his disapproval. She wondered that her ladyship should choose to take a journey when Lord Veryan must be expected shortly from Stannisburn, but that, after all, was none of her business.

By one o'clock Katharine was as ready as she could hope to be, and, after rather anxiously adding up what remained of her quarterly allowance — if only she had not bought that new bonnet! — allowed herself to be bowed into the waiting carriage. She left no message for her husband, nor any indication of when she would return, merely instructing the butler to inform all interested parties that she was sojourning with the Duke of Clayre at Cheard, near Bath.

10

THE room was small, and dimly lit. An uncorked brandy bottle stood in solitary state on a rough wooden table, about which sat three men, glasses in hand. The door opened, and three pairs of eyes were raised expectantly. Mr. Waterhouse was in the doorway, and cast a supercilious glance at the occupants. Slowly he entered the room and shut the door with a sharp click. A branch of candles stood on the low sideboard, and he caught these up, placing them strategically beside the brandy bottle so that the flicker lit the faces of the three men, casting the rest of the room into darkness.

"I do not suppose," he said, idly flicking open his snuff-box, "that you have found him?"

The men shifted uncomfortably on

their hard wooden chairs. For a moment no one spoke, and then one, the largest of the three, a pugilist whose face had clearly seen better days, raised his eyes fleetingly to his employer's face and said unnecessarily: "'E ain't at Stannisburn."

Mr. Waterhouse's thin upper lip curled. "Naturally he is not. He is here, in London. He has been seen, but not, I fear, by any of you."

"I went to Kensington, like you said," volunteered a bald, toothless individual suddenly, "but 'e's lying low. There's no findin' 'im, guvnor."

Mr. Waterhouse's eyes flickered. "He is there, so he may be found. What of you, Joshua? Where were you?"

The third man seemed uncomfortable. "Followed 'er la'ship, guvnor. No luck there neither. 'E never came near the place, an' she certainly din't go to Kensington." He cast a glance at his employer, then lowered his eyes quickly. Mr. Waterhouse, half hidden in shadow, carefully returned the snuff box to his pocket and regarded them with dislike.

"Since a man cannot vanish, he must still be here. However, since you have so far failed, and I concede that perhaps it was not entirely through ineptitude, we must force him into the open. He is dangerous, gentlemen, and frightened. He must be traced, and swiftly." He paused, and moved towards the table. "There is a way. Her ladyship has gone to Bath, to Cheard. She is not dangerous, and is not hiding. The wife is the key to the husband. You will go to Bath, you will take the wife, and the husband will come to us. It is easy. My only worry is that you will not be able to execute your parts. However," and his eyes flickered again, "I know you will try your best, as did Mr. Davis."

The mention of their deceased companion caused an exchange of glances, and a pair of feet shuffled beneath the table. The pugilist cleared his throat.

"How do we get 'er away, guvnor? She's not likely to come wiv us."

"Naturally not. I shall encourage her into the coach on some pretext. Then you, who will be posing as coachman, groom, and outrider, will apparently turn on us, throwing me into the ditch, to all appearances dead. You will then conceal her, while I, apparently suffering from shock, convey the news to London. It will reach the husband with ease."

"'Ow do we know 'e'll come?" asked the pugilist, Henry, eyeing his employer dubiously.

"He'll come, that is certain. Then we hand him to the law. Justice will serve our purpose."

"Look 'ere, guvnor," said Henry suddenly, setting down his empty glass, "why can't we pop 'im off, like, nice an' simple? That way there's no chance of 'im talking, see."

"It may yet come to that, my friend; have patience. Do not slip up, and you will be well rewarded."

* * *

Henry Jicks, the broad gentleman with a squashed nose and lace edged ear, was worried. Mr. Waterhouse had long since departed, leaving him and his companions to contemplate the plot over several more glasses of rough brandy. Now Joshua and Jacob were gone too, and Henry was left to his thoughts. These were not happy. The fate of Mr. Davis still haunted him, and he began to think that he had been mistaken to get involved with such a cunning and ruthless gentleman as Mr. Waterhouse. So far, his part in the proceedings had been limited to a fruitless journey into Hampshire, and following Lady Veryan about town, an occupation as undemanding as it was boring. Mr. Davis had been the partner in crime, and Mr. Davis was dead. Henry had no desire to wind up similarly defunct. He knew perfectly well that the kidnapping of a lady of society was a risky operation, and one that would necessarily result in the gallows for the likes of him. His mental processes were not quick, but it did not take him many minutes to realize that there was only one way Mr. Waterhouse would feel safe, and that was with him, Jacob, and old Joshua costly nailed up in neat boxes. The more he thought about it, the plainer it seemed. Mr. Waterhouse was no man to leave loose ends, and loose ends he, Jacob, and Joshua would most certainly be. It was not a happy reflection. By ten o'clock he was very concerned indeed, and, with the worthy intention of blowing away some of the cobwebs that clouded his brain, he went outside for a walk.

It is uncertain what drew him to Grosvenor Square, but it is likely that his feet trod their accustomed course, and within a half hour he found himself staring up at the elegant residence of the Marquis of Veryan. For a moment he was confused, and stood on the pavement wondering what he should do. As he pondered a carriage appeared from the direction of South Audley Street, and he pressed himself into the shadows for fear of being seen. The carriage was proceeding slowly, and in a moment had drawn up before Clayre House. As Henry watched a gentleman in evening dress descended and ran lightly up the steps to pull the bell. Holding his breath fearfully Henry strained his large ears for some snippet of conversation.

Mr. Malling stamped his feet impatiently. It was cold outside, and the cursed butler was taking an unconscionable time in opening the door. At last footsteps sounded, however, and Mr. Malling breathed a sigh of relief.

"Oh, good evening, Lowell," he said cheerfully as the door was opened. "Is her la'ship in?"

"I regret to say, sir, that the Marchioness departed three days ago for Somersetshire, and is not expected back for several days."

Mr. Malling looked nonplussed. "Oh. I say, are you sure? I mean, if she's just not seeing anybody, could you tell her I have a message from his lordship, the Marquis?"

"I am sorry, sir, her ladyship is out of town. Goodnight, sir." The door was slowly, but firmly shut. Mr. Malling turned, and thoughtfully descended to the street. At that moment Henry, who had heard all that he needed, made what was, for him, a snap decision, and stepped out of the shadows to address Mr. Malling. Unfortunately his intentions were misunderstood. Mr. Malling, seeing a large and fearful-looking individual bearing down upon him, raised his cane above his head and said loudly: "Don't come any nearer or I strike!"

Henry was startled. This was not what he expected. "'Ere wait, guvnor, I ain't no thief! I mean, I ain't no thief of *you*, guvnor. I must have words!"

Mr. Malling, realizing that perhaps this enormous pugilist did not mean to hit him, rob him, and leave him for dead, slowly lowered his cane, and regarded the fellow suspiciously. "Just what do you want, my man?"

The cane was lowered, but Mr. Malling still grasped it tightly, and for a moment each regarded the other warily. At last Henry lowered his eyes and rubbed his nose thoughtfully.

"I need to speak to 'is lordship. Private, like. Important to 'im an' 'is lady."

"Indeed! Important in what way?"

"I discuss that wiv 'is lordship," responded Henry stubbornly.

"Well, now, just why should I take you to see Lord Veryan? How do I know what you intend by him?"

For a moment Henry regarded him uncomprehendingly, then he said: "My guvnor, Mr. Waterhouse, is planning something that ain't to 'is lordship's advantage; You take me to 'im. I'll talk to 'im only."

Mr. Malling looked stunned. Here, it seemed, stood an employee of Mr.

Waterhouse, apparently with information to impart. The possibility of a trap could not but suggest itself. He eyed the fellow thoughtfully. "Where is Mr. Waterhouse now?"

"Gawd luv yer, I dunno! Look, 'ere, I ain't got no time to talk wiv you. I've to go to Bath in the mornin', an' I must see 'is lordship now!"

Mr. Malling decided to take a chance. As far as he could see the street was deserted, and it was not an opportunity he could afford to miss. Accordingly he nodded to his coachman who held open the door of the carriage for them to enter. In a moment the coachman had whipped up his horses and started slowly down the street. Mr. Malling positioned himself with his back to the coachman so that he had a clear view of the street behind them. As far as he could tell, they were not followed. Standing up, he poked his head out of the window.

"Kensington, William, fast."

A grunt, and the horses were whipped

up. Mr. Malling, somewhat tardy in regaining his seat, was thrown from one side of the carriage to the other. Henry gave him an uninterested glance, then returned to his contemplation of his thick fingers.

The house in Plexham Gardens was shabbily genteel, and never failed to depress Mr. Malling as he stepped into the dim hall. The carpets were worn and sent a dull echo to the top of the stair well as they climbed. As they reached the landing Mr. Malling cast a speculative glance at his companion, and then sighed, and rapped smartly on an oak-panelled door. There was silence for a moment, then a voice, pregnant with suspicion, called out sharply: "Who is it?"

"It's me, Ver, Freddie. Let me in."

There came the sound of a chair being pushed back, then footsteps sounded across a bare floor. A key grated and the door was thrown open. Lord Veryan turned without a glance at his visitor and walked back to the table. A half-empty bottle of wine awaited him. Mr. Malling nodded to his companion and they entered the room, Henry Jicks carefully closing the door. The Marquis was again seated at the table, and Mr. Malling noticed with concern that his colour was high and his eye bright.

"I've brought someone to see you, Ver."

The dark head jerked up, and the clouded gaze focused with difficulty on the large man. "What the devil — ?" he ejaculated half-rising in his chair.

"Take it easy, Ver," said Mr. Malling, laying a hand on his friend's shoulder. "Believe it or not, I think this fellow is our stroke of luck. I found him loitering in Grosvenor Square. He was damned keen to speak to you, I must say."

There was a distinct menace in the Marquis's blue eyes, but he relaxed in his chair and regarded the fellow silently.

"He works for George," explained Mr. Malling.

The Marquis, reluctantly transferring his gaze from one guest to the other, looked at Mr. Malling scornfully. "I suppose it has occurred to you that this might be a trap. George might be outside at this very minute."

"No 'e ain't," said Henry suddenly, taking a couple of purposeful steps towards the Marquis. "And I ain't come 'ere ter chatter neither."

Lord Veryan raised a brow. "Just why are you here, friend? And why were you loitering in Grosvenor Square?"

Mr. Jicks frowned. "I was thinking, see. The guv-nor give us orders, an' I dint like 'em. So I went to the Square, like, jest in case you was there. An' I found this cove instead."

"I see. Just what do you want with me?"

"Protection, guvnor. 'E's a bad lot, is Mr. Waterhouse, that 'e is. 'E did for old Jim, right enough, an' Jim never did nothing agin 'is worship neither."

Lord Veryan sat up straight. "You know he killed that man? Will you swear to it if necessary?"

"Ah, now, as to that I dunno. I might, an' I might not. It depen's."

"On what, exactly?"

"On what protection you give me."

The Marquis looked thoughtful. "I see. I think you had better tell me what you know."

"An' the protection, guvnor?"

"Well, as to that, I don't know, I'm afraid. But if I understand your position correctly you're afraid Mr. Waterhouse will kill you when you have done the work, or even if you don't. So whatever help I can give must be worthwhile, must it not?"

Henry looked sullen and unconvinced. "I dunno. I ain't done nothing wrong, yet, yesee, guvnor, an' I ain't of a mind to start *now*."

"You must have been at one time," Lord Veryan pointed out logically.

Mr. Jicks reddened slightly. "Ay, well, that was afore Jim caught it."

"Very well. Tell us what you know, and we'll do what we can. I'm afraid you'll have to be satisfied with that, my friend. You must know the Law is after me."

"Ah now." Mr. Jicks tapped his nose significantly. "That's what I want to talk to you about, guvnor."

"Well, sit down, Mr — er — "

"Jicks."

" — Mr. Jicks, and tell me."

Henry pulled up a chair, and sitting down, examined his fingers thoughtfully. "It's to do wiv your good lady," he said at last.

"My wife? How so?"

"Seeing as how she's at Bath, like," explained Mr. Jicks helpfully.

"At Bath!" exploded Lord Veryan, pushing back his chair violently. "How is it you failed to mention this, Freddie?"

Mr. Malling reddened, and started to speak, but Henry cut him short.

"Now see 'ere, guvnor, either you listen, or I go to Bow Street." Lord

240

Veryan eyed him with loathing, and seated himself again. "Mr. Waterhouse, see, 'e wants to come by your whereabouts mortal bad. But 'e can't find yer, see. So 'e hits on the plan to take 'er ladyship, so as you come running, straight into 'is arms. Simple, like." He beamed cheerfully at his two stunned auditors.

"Good God!" said Mr. Malling, staring at his friend's shocked countenance.

Lord Veryan sat very quiet for a minute or two, then turned to Mr. Jicks, his expression grave. "When is this planned *for*, Mr. Jicks?"

"We leaves Lunnon early, like, in the morning, sharpish."

"Now listen. I want you to go, just as planned. No, don't interrupt. Say nothing to Mr. Waterhouse of our little talk. I shall leave for Bath tonight, and warn her ladyship. Then when you come, all we have to do is collect Mr. Waterhouse and turn him over to the Authorities. You, Freddie, will go to Bow Street. You will get as many Runners as you can to Cheard on whatever pretext you like. Tell them I'm hiding there if you must. Then you, Mr. Jicks, will testify against Mr. Waterhouse, and if all goes well I'll find you a position in my household. Will that suit?"

Mr. Jicks considered, rubbing his stubbly chin ruminatively. "Well, it ain't perfect, that it ain't. However, it'll do. I ain't daft. Mr. Waterrouse'll find it 'ard to spill my claret an' that's a *fact*!" He grinned toothlessly at his companions.

"Yes, well, you had better run along, Mr. Jicks, before you're missed. You'd better give me a ride to Clayre House, Freddie. I hope her ladyship hasn't taken my carriage, that's all."

11

LORD VERYAN parted from his friend at Clayre House, and ran quickly up the steps to the front door. It was past twelve and the house was plunged in darkness. It was, therefore, several minutes before a scuffle sounded behind the locked and bolted door, and it was drawn back, revealing a tousled individual in a night-cap. His jaw dropped as he saw his master, and he stepped back quickly.

"I beg your pardon, my lord," he said hurriedly, supremely conscious of his dishevelled appearance, "but I did not know to expect you! I hope your lorship will excuse my appearance."

"Rouse Joseph at once," said his lordship, grasping the butler's single candle with barely a glance. "Tell him to have the chaise ready in ten

minutes. Send Peeble to my room."
He had by now gained the stairway
and ran up two stairs at a time,
leaving Lowell to put his orders into
bewildered execution.

Lord Veryan found his room depress-
ingly tidy, and for a moment stood in
the doorway with the candle casting an
inadequate light into the room. Then
he marched inside and applied the weak
flame to several other candles within the
room. Peeble was an orderly servant
and Lord Veryan, after looking briefly
into several cupboards and drawers,
realized that he was not going to find
what he wanted without his valet's
assistance. Consequently he perched
on the smooth bed and passed the few
minutes by drumming his heels into
the thick carpet. Peeble appeared with
a rapidity that did him credit, since he
had been in bed for almost two hours,
but was soundly scolded for keeping his
master waiting. He had, in fact, dressed
in a very great hurry, and was only glad
that the light in the room was such

that his hastiness was not immediately apparent to his master.

"Where have you put my pistols?" demanded his lordship, once more throwing open a cupboard and performing a futile search.

"They are in the chest in your dressing room, my lord. Shall I fetch them?"

"Yes. Powder and balls too. And my sword, if you can find it. I only hope it's clean."

The valet disappeared, returning in a very short time with a long black case and a slim sword in a leather scabbard.

"Thank you, Peeble. I suppose it does help to be tidy, but I wish to heaven I knew where you kept my things." Fumbling a little, he fastened the sword about his waist beneath the coat, then examined the pair of pistols that Peeble displayed to him. "Good. I can load them on the way. You're a good fellow, Peeble. Go back to bed. I shan't need you."

Clasping the black box tightly, Lord Veryan hurried down the stairs again, only to find that the coach was not yet ready. Lowell, who had dressed, apologised profusely, and ventured to say that if they had known his lordship would be needing the carriage he would not have been kept waiting. The remark went unheard.

In a few minutes, however, wheels could be heard before the front door, and Lord Veryan hurried out. The coachman, Joseph, attempted to apologise by saying that one of the leaders had objected to being put to at that time of night, but they were nevertheless quite fresh and would make good time. Scarcely heeding him, Lord Veryan climbed into the carriage and ordered them to Cheard, with the instructions to put up for a change as often as was necessary. "I've no mind for delays, Joseph, so when the horses get tired, don't push them. But take them to Slough if you can."

Joseph clambered onto his box and exchanged glances with the groom, then the horses were whipped up and trotted off down the street.

It was a little before one when the light chaise left London, and, apart from an occasional carriage bearing its occupant home after an evening's entertainment the roads were clear. The horses were very fresh, and needed no encouragement to make a good pace. The carriage swung and rattled its way out of London with almost startling abandon.

Lord Veryan paid little attention to the passing miles. He reclined with his eyes closed and his legs along the padded seat, trying to see off the last of the clouds that were fuddling his brain. His evening had been one of solitary indulgence. He had drunk several glasses of wine, two of port and two of brandy, and when Mr. Malling called, had found it difficult to collect his thoughts sufficiently for action. Now, a clear head was essential. He knew perfectly well what lay ahead, and the prospect of two Mr. Waterhouses dancing in front of him was not one that appealed.

The horses covered the twenty or so miles to Slough in a little over an hour and a half, and came to a halt sweating and steaming in the yard of the Crown Inn. It was a little while before anyone appeared, night travellers, apart from the Mail, being rare, but Lord Veryan had only just begun to think that their quest was useless when a tousle-headed and sleepy-eyed ostler appeared in answer to the groom's summons. A few minutes later and the landlord himself arrived, willing to put himself to extra trouble for the heir to a dukedom. All offers of refreshment were, however, declined, although the Marquis did say that two tankards of best ale might be brought for his groom and coachman. The Marquis's generosity to the ostler and landlord resulted in four well-matched animals being put within the traces, the whole operation taking just a little over ten minutes.

Another hour and a quarter saw them at Reading. The horses from the Crown had proved excellent and fast, and had another stage existed five miles further they might have accomplished it with ease. But the next stage was Newbury, another seventeen miles, so the change must be made now.

The landlord of the Angel did not prove so obliging. He complained heartily at being aroused at four o'clock on a harsh February morning, and in spite of the large fee offered him seemed reluctant even to rouse the ostlers. The weary horses were relieved eventually, however, and the chaise rolled out of the yard after a delay of nearly half an hour.

The new horses were slow, and the pace considerably lessened by their inability to obey the commands of the coachman. The seventeen miles took nearly two hours to complete, and the Marquis arrived at Newbury heartily sick of the Angel Inn.

The Marquis partook of breakfast at Marlborough. He had intended to press on without delay, but since Mr. Waterhouse was not due to leave London until the morning he decided to answer the demands of his stomach. Having eaten, the Marquis decided that a wash and a shave was in order, and, with this purpose in mind, hired a room for an hour or so. One glance at his reflection in the mirror confirmed his worst fears. He was still dressed in his clothes of the day before, and, since he had taken little trouble over his appearance whilst in Kensington, the sight was sufficiently terrible to make him wince and call loudly for the servant. There was no way that he could appear at Cheard dressed as he was. It was barely ten o'clock; Waterhouse would hardly have started. Accordingly he sent the servant for hot water and lay back on the bed to await his return.

This was his mistake. The servant,

returning a few minutes later, discovered his lordship reclining full-length on the bed, apparently dead to the world. Having had no answer to his knock he had opened the door quietly and stood for a moment observing the motionless body. To rouse the heir to a dukedom was, as far as he was concerned, unthinkable, so, having placed the jug and bowl on the chest of drawers he withdrew and pulled the door closed behind him. He then hurried downstairs and proceeded to forget about it.

Two hours later there was an arrival. Sir Edward Carradale and his two companions had passed the night at Newbury, and, now that it was well past noon, had decided to stop at the George for a light luncheon.

Sir Edward was a rotund gentleman with a balding head and florid countenance. It had grieved him to be forced to depart as early as nine o'clock, for he was never an early riser, and had lingered over-long with his port the night before. But his companions were in a hurry. Time was important, and they had no mind to let the rather unattractive Sir Edward delay them longer than was necessary. Consequently, Sir Edward had been summoned before eight, and had been put to such exigencies that he thought at one point he would die of an apoplexy before even reaching his destination. It was with great relief that he sank into a deep armchair in the coffee room and received a pint of ale from the servant. He was beginning to feel a little better. His companions had taken themselves to the tap room, for which he was profoundly grateful, it being bad enough to be forced to share his carriage with them. There was a fire blazing in the grate, too, which would have been warming had not that fool of a servant left the door ajar. For several minutes Sir Edward endured the draught that crept in and swept about his legs, then he sighed, set down his tankard, and heaved himself to his feet. Making his way across the room he became aware of a conversation taking place just down the corridor. Now, while Sir Edward did not regard himself as an inquisitive man, one thing he delighted in was the conversation of others. A very few words, however, satisfied him that it was merely the talk of menials, and he was closing the door when a name caught his ear and caused him to stay his hand.

"Look, it's more than my position's worth to rouse a Marquis when he's sleeping. He may be your master, but he's paying for his room, and that's where he stays while I'm landlord. Now get about your business."

"I'm telling you, aren't I? The Marquis will skin me for letting him sleep so long, when we travelled all night just to get there quick! He wanted to be at Cheard afore noon, told me so himself, and he certainly had no thoughts of sleeping, that I do know."

"Well, however that may be, it's not

my place to wake him. Now be off."

There followed a pause, during which Sir Edward acted. Pulling open the door, he rapidly discerned the two men, and, with his corsets creaking slightly, made his ponderous way towards them.

"My man," he began, addressing the landlord importantly, "do I understand you to be referring to the Marquis of Veryan?"

The landlord, casting a darkling look at the coachman, bowed, and said: "Yes, sir. But do not concern yourself. It is no important matter."

"On the contrary. I believe this fellow is anxious to awaken his master. Let me assist you. I am his lordship's cousin, Sir Edward Carradale. I shall be happy to awaken him."

The landlord smiled. "Why, sir, we would be very grateful. You understand it is not customary for us to disturb our guests, but if you are his *cousin* . . . It is the first door on the left at the top of the stairs. The servant will show you."

Sir Edward raised a hand. "It is of no consequence. I shall find my way."

He turned, and in a moment was mounting the stairway to the first floor. At the top he hesitated, then turned left and stopped at the first floor he came to. For a moment he waited, an expression of concentration on his florid face, listening intently. Satisfied that no sound was emanating from the room he cautiously turned the handle and peered in. The Marquis was still soundly sleeping, lying full-length on the bed, his clothes crumpled beneath him, and snoring very slightly. Sir Edward could hardly believe his luck. He had come into the country on intuition. No sooner had the news reached him that his cousin had not only vanished, but was wanted in Bow Street than he set about tracing the missing heir. A murder charge was better than he could ever have hoped, and the prospect of the dukedom at once grew a little clearer. It had taken little imagination to determine where his lordship must be, and it had needed only the information that Lady Veryan had departed into Somersetshire to spur him into action. Shutting the door quietly he retreated to the stairs, and in a moment had found his way to the tap-room.

Lord Veryan sat up, and glanced quickly round. The impression that someone was in the room had been strong enough to jerk him out of deep slumber, and it did not immediately fade. He relaxed, however, and ran a hand through his ruffled hair. For a moment he had no recollection of his previous movements, of his reason for being where he was, and what he should do now, then his eye fell on the plain white jug that still reposed on the chest of drawers. With a curse he swung his feet to the floor, poured the now cold water from the jug into the shallow bowl, and hurriedly splashed it over his face. Grumbling still he ripped the crumpled neck-cloth from about his throat, glanced round for the mirror, and started rearranging his cravat.

During his weeks in Kensington, Lord Veryan had trained himself to be alert for every eventuality. It had resulted in his jumping nervously whenever the faithful Mr. Malling had climbed the stairs, and now he felt the hair on the back of his neck rising before he even realized he had heard the board creak. Sharp footsteps would not have disturbed him, for what is more natural in an inn? But the creak of a floor-board and the suggestion of a sibilant whisper set every nerve tingling in his body. In a flash he had discovered the position of every piece of furniture in the room, had shifted his sword slightly, and had discovered that the only window was too small for him to jump through. Even as the handle was moving he hid himself behind the door and carefully drew his sword from its scabbard.

Two men entered the room together. They were both broad, and dressed in buff breeches and jackets. They had run into the room, but seeing the bed empty hesitated, then swung round. A sword, bright and shining, confronted them, and they found themselves staring at a tall, loose-limbed gentleman with tousled brown hair and strangely bright blue eyes.

"Forgive me, gentlemen, if I don't stay." So saying, Lord Veryan swept a circle before him with his sword, and with his left hand jerked away the mat upon which one conveniently had both feet, and the other one. The larger of the two fell back heavily, catching his arm on the table and oversetting the water-jug. The other slid in the direction of the bed. Lord Veryan did not wait. He rounded the door, and immediately collided with something that was large and soft and fell panting against the opposite wall. With a half-laugh Lord Veryan recognised his winded cousin, then he was running down the stairs and out of the inn.

Joseph had been waiting some time

for his master, and the horses had been poled up for an hour or more. With a start he recognised the figure rushing from the inn, and hurriedly removed the straw from his mouth.

"Get up, Joseph, for the devil's sake!"

Beckoning urgently to the lounging groom, Joseph swung himself into the box and whipped up the horses as his master wrenched open the carriage door and fell inside. The carriage lurched and bumped out of the yard, and Lord Veryan, struggling to his feet, saw a red-faced landlord waving his fists in the doorway. He had forgotten to pay his shot.

12

SIR EDWARD CARRADALE was feeling very ill-used. Lord Veryan had cannoned into him at full speed, and his resulting crash against the passage wall had done little good for the roast beef and ale he had consumed at breakfast. Then on top of this while he was still panting on the passage floor the two Runners had had the impudence to suggest that he, Sir Edward Carradale, had been responsible for the whole thing, and, moreover, that if he did not make haste they would have no scruples about leaving him behind. But even this was not all. Battered and bruised, he had staggered down the stairs, only to be greeted by a furious landlord demanding that he pay the Marquis's shot. Expostulation had been useless. He had himself informed the fellow of his close relations with the Marquis, and the landlord had made it quite plain that if he did not pay he would not be allowed to remove his carriage from the yard. So he had paid, and his feelings for his errant cousin could hardly have been less cordial.

Now, seated in his chaise once more, he had time, at least, to enumerate his wrongs. But these seemed to grow with every minute. His companions had smelt their quarry, and had no intention of letting him slip. They gave every indication of putting up a determined chase. The larger of the two, a fellow named Faul, had actually had the impudence to lean out of the window and instruct Sir Edward's coachman to 'spring 'em'. Uttering a groan, Sir Edward closed his eyes and prayed fervently that they might overtake the Marquis before his breakfast gave an account of itself.

It was barely five minutes before the elderly coachman gave a cry that signified the Marquis's coach. Until now the road had been wide and relatively straight, but a hill was approaching and once the summit had been gained the road came notoriously winding and narrow. Nevertheless the coachman made a determined effort. It was many years since he had been given the chance to race another chaise, Sir Edward's preferred pace being slow and stately. Now, he laid his whips into the backs of the horses and gave a loud halloo. The horses responded faithfully. As the Marquis's chaise began climbing the hill they started to gain, and the coachman shouted once more. Whipping his horses the faster, he set them into the foot of the hill and they panted valiantly up it. But Sir Edward's chaise was heavy. Not only did it carry two extra persons, but it was laden with Sir Edward's bags and boxes. The Marquis's chaise reached the summit and disappeared. Spurred by the excitement of the chase the elderly coachman encouraged greater speed out of his weary horses and mounted the summit also. He had barely time to see that the Marquis's chaise had pulled onto the grass before the sharp descent of the hill caught the carriage and it began rolling down the other side. The quantity of baggage and the three heavy passengers gave it momentum. The horses, glad to find the load relieved, plunged recklessly into the descent. Too late the coachman realized his mistake. He heaved on the brake, but to no avail. Soon, too, the horses felt the weight of the carriage behind them and began to panic. Their eyes staring and nostrils flared they hurtled down the hill, until they reached the bottom and with it grief. A wheel caught a boulder; before either coachman or horses knew the danger the carriage overturned and was dragged along the ground on its side. The coachman and groom were flung clear, and after a few moments the horses, finding a much increased weight behind them, came to a shambling standstill, and stood panting and snorting on the grass.

A few hundred yards behind the Marquis had watched the whole incident. Sitting back in the chaise he banged on the roof, and the carriage moved off slowly. As they approached the scene of the crash the horses slowed to a walk, and the Marquis peered out. A strange sight greeted him. Sir Edward's face appeared through the window. He was a sickly green colour, and for a moment seemed unaware of what had happened. Then his eye fell on his cousin, and his expression rapidly took on a purple hue. Chuckling to himself, the Marquis banged on the roof, and the carriage moved forward once more.

From then on the journey was uneventful. Such was his respect for the aristocracy and for heirs to dukedom's in particular, that the landlord of the inn had ordered his best team to be poled up and they made excellent time. The final change was made at Chippenham and Lord Veryan, climbing back into the chaise after examining the road for the ten minutes it took to change the teams, instructed Joseph to strike onto the Lacock road and approach Bath from the south. At half past three the Bath road was heavy with traffic, besides which the Cheard estate bordered Bath on the south side and they would therefore avoid the town.

It was past five o'clock when Cheard Lodge came in view and the carriage negotiated the awkward turn into the South Avenue. Had he had the time or leisure, the Marquis might have observed the stark beauty of the bare trees, but his mind was wholly fixed on the house ahead and until he knew Katharine to be safe he could not rest.

The door opened as the carriage halted, and a liveried footman hurried out. "Stay here, Joseph," said the Marquis curtly, descending onto the stones, "there may yet be work for you. See that my servants have some refreshment, if you please!" The footman bowed and Lord Veryan ran into the house. He was met by John, descending the staircase slowly, and waited impatiently until he reached the bottom.

"Well, John, take me to my wife. Where is she?"

John carefully looked surprised. "Lady Veryan, my lord? I am afraid your lordship is mistaken. Lady Veryan departed yesterday."

It was a reply the Marquis had half-expected. "Dammit, man do you think I don't know she's here? I haven't come all the way from town to be fobbed off like this, I can tell you!"

"I assure you, my lord, Lady Veryan is not at Cheard. However, if you wish to see his Grace, I am sure he will be willing to receive you."

"Damn your eyes, John!" exclaimed the Marquis irascible. "Lead on, then."

Whatever his impatience, Lord Veryan submitted to the formality preferred by his Grace, and therefore followed the servant up the stairs and along the passage to his Grace's apartment. John's pace, however, was slow enough to put all the Marquis's self control to the test, and when he was finally ushered in he felt his temper rising dangerously. Scarcely waiting for the servant to go he burst out: "Where's Katharine, Duke? I know she's here, and it's so damned important I've been travelling all night!"

The old Duke's gaze calmly took in his heir's appearance. He was seated in a deep winged chair, his back to the light, but although Lord Veryan could not distinguish his expression, he instinctively raised a hand to the cravat he had never finished tying.

"You are mistaken," the duke said shortly. "She left yesterday to visit her cousins in Bristol."

"Bristol? What cousins? She's got no cousins in Bristol!"

"On the contrary. She is visiting them now."

For a moment Lord Veryan glared at the old man, then took two rapid paces and dropped into the nearest chair. "Look here, Duke, I have to find her.

It's desperate, or I would not be here at all. If she really is in Bristol give me her direction. I'll find her there."

There was a short pause, then his Grace stood up slowly and walked across the room. A door stood open a little way, and he went through into an adjoining chamber, shutting the door carefully behind him. Lord Veryan stood up and began pacing impatiently. After what seemed an hour, but was in truth a little under five minutes, the Duke reappeared with a folded paper. "This is it. You'd better take it, I suppose."

Impatiently Lord Veryan grasped the paper, and hastily read the duke's spidery writing. Dropping it onto the table he grinned suddenly and said: "With luck I shall bring her back. Prepare our rooms, would you?"

"Ha!" The old man glared at his grandson, then without another word waved his hand and sat back down in the chair. Lord Veryan grinned again, and was gone.

For a minute or more his Grace of Clayre sat motionless in his chair, his face expressionless in the shadow. Then he rose and began absently to finger the paper his grandson had dropped. Into the silence came the sound of hooves and wheels, and when this noise had faded to nothing he turned and said:

"Come, child, he has gone."

The door to the adjoining room opened slowly and Katharine, pale and troubled, entered the room and eyed her protector thoughtfully. She attempted a laugh. "Well, I am glad of that at least. Tell me, did he seem very put out?"

"He looked as though he had not slept for a week," responded the Duke with a twinkle. "His hair was untidy, his cravat disgraceful, and yes, my dear, he was vastly put out. In fact, he was very nearly rude to me! Now why didn't I notice that before? On retrospect I would say he was more put out than I suspected. I have never known him to be even *almost* rude before! Indeed, Katty, you have done him a great deal of good."

She gave a wry smile. "Because he was rude to you?"

"Because he no longer cared what I thought of him. Do you know, I really believe if I had told him I would cut him off he would not have cared a fig! In fact, I rather suspect he would have laughed at me! He must be very much in love with you, my dear."

Katharine laughed. "With me, grandpapa? Indeed he is not! I only wish he were, but it is Elizabeth he wants, not me."

The Duke looked at her from beneath his shaggy white brows. "Child, so far I have listened patiently to you, but I really think it is time you were reasonable. Do you seriously think he would make a mad dash all this way, travelling over night, too, if he did not care for you? It does not sound like Christopher to me."

"Sir, there was a time when I would have been delighted to hear you say such a thing, but I know it is not true. I left London because I discovered him actually in my brother's house, hiding in the next room, as a matter of fact."

The Duke chuckled, and even Katharine was betrayed into giggling. "Poor Christopher! I suppose you didn't give him a chance to explain? No, of course you didn't. Just rushed out of the house without another thought."

Katharine looked a little guilty, but said nothing.

"And this murder business. Surely you do not believe him capable of that?"

"Of course I do not!" Katharine exclaimed indignantly. "I hope I am not so unfair!"

"Yet you believe him capable of marrying you so as to be near your sister."

Katharine looked struck.

The Duke cast her a sly glance, and rubbed his chin thoughtfully. "I wonder just what did bring him here in such a rush," he said, musingly.

For a moment Katharine gave no sign of having heard, and then of a sudden she looked up, her eyes widening a little. "Do you really think it was something important?"

"Well, my dear, he called me 'Duke', which is something he has not done in his life."

"Good Heavens! Grandpapa, do you think those dreadful Runners are after him?"

"Katty, my dear, you should not call our admirable Runners dreadful, but it would not surprise me in the least to discover he had half a dozen or so on his tail."

"And I sent him on to Bristol! Heavens, what have I done!"

"I should think, my dear, that you have considerably increased his chances of being caught," responded the old gentleman, rather unfairly. But Katharine looked horrified.

"Oh, how dreadful I am! I didn't

even give him a chance to tell me what he wanted! I must go after him at once, sir; will you lend me your carriage?"

"With the greatest of pleasure, my dear," replied the Duke, pleased with himself.

The sound of hooves came from below, and Katharine, thinking it might be the Marquis, hurried to the window and peered out. She was just about to turn away in disappointment when a familiar figure caught her eye. "Oh, it's George! Grandfather, it's Mr. Waterhouse! He'll help me, I do know."

Beyond raising a brow at her enthusiasm, the Duke passed no comment on the arrival of a stranger at his door, or on Katharine's hurried quittal of his presence. But he rose, and calmly walked to the window that overlooked the avenue.

As she ran downstairs Katharine had little idea of what she should do, and it was only as she gained the hall and watched John opening the door that the idea came to her. Hurrying past the surprised butler she ran outside, to the astonishment of Mr. Waterhouse, who had been about to mount the steps.

"Oh, George! How glad I am you are here! You are the very person I need! Do come inside and have some refreshment. John, some wine for Mr. Waterhouse."

The bemused John bowed and moved away as Katharine caught Mr. Waterhouse's arm and drew him into the ground floor parlour.

"George, this is a great surprise! How did you know I was here?"

Mr. Waterhouse smiled. "You left word with your butler, my dear, or had you forgot?"

"No, of course not. Tell me, have you come all this way just to see me, or have you business in Bath?"

The brilliant eyes sparkled. "I should like to say I am here solely for a glimpse of you, but I'm afraid it would not be wholly true. I have a business matter to settle too, I must admit."

"Oh dear. Well I hope it won't be too dull for you. Tell me, George, have you travelled far today?"

Mr. Waterhouse, who had in fact left London a little before six that morning, replied: "Only from Hungerford. We stopped over for the night."

"Oh. Because George, I am wondering if you could do something for me."

"Anything, if I can."

"I have to go to Bristol, at once. Would you escort me, please, in your carriage? It really is most urgent, or I can assure you I would never think of asking such a thing of you."

"To Bristol, my dear? But what business have you there?"

"I have to visit some cousins. It really is very important I get there tonight. Please, George. His Grace will change your horses, and it won't take much above an hour! If we leave now we could be there by seven."

Mr. Waterhouse looked amused. "And these cousins of yours, will they give us dinner? I should hate to go so far without even a morsel."

"Well, to be honest, I'm not certain about that, but there will be plenty of places for us to eat in Bristol if they do not."

"I hope so, indeed! But tell me, Katharine, had I better not pay my respects to the Duke? It seems hardly proper to leave before I have even arrived!"

"Oh, John will explain, won't you, John?" The servant had entered just then with a bottle and two glasses. "Mr. Waterhouse has kindly offered to escort me to Bristol and we must leave at once. You will explain to Grandfather, won't you? I hope to be back before tonight, and perhaps a chamber could be prepared for Mr. Waterhouse."

"Certainly, my lady. Will you be requiring the wine?"

"Yes," replied Mr. Waterhouse firmly, before Katharine could refuse. "I shall partake of some while you fetch your wrap, Katharine."

It was not yet six o'clock when the travelling carriage set out again on its unexpected journey to Bristol. Mr. Waterhouse, leaning comfortably against the padded seat, had no difficulty in deciding what was the purpose of Katharine's sudden journey, and could only marvel that fate had thus played into his hands. He watched Katharine in the other corner as she eagerly scanned the road ahead and became certain that they had embarked on a pursuit of the very person he was wishful to catch. On two occasions he attempted to induce Katharine into conversation. The first time she ignored him completely, and he suspected she had not heard, being engaged in peering forward into the gloom. On the second occasion she turned her head and said: "I beg your pardon, but do you hear a chaise up ahead?"

Mr. Waterhouse smiled. "I think, my lady, that you had better tell me what you are up to. Are we chasing someone, for example?"

Katharine stared at him, then laughed. "I am sorry! How rude I am to snub you! You are quite right. I should have told you, I know, especially since you are such a good friend. My husband came to see me today, and I . . . I was stupid enough to send him away without seeing him. Well, now I've changed my mind. I hope you don't mind my not telling you, George, but it is true that we are going to cousins of mine. At least, that's where I sent Christopher, though what they will say if he gets there first I can't imagine, since I haven't heard from them for ten years or more!"

Mr. Waterhouse looked amused. "Then we had better make all the haste we can." Leaning from the carriage he shouted instructions, and in a moment the horses had been whipped up to a greater speed.

"This is really very kind of you, George," said Katharine, smiling on him warmly. "I'm sure Christopher does not realize what a good friend he has in you."

"I am sure he will appreciate me fully after today," responded Mr. Waterhouse, comfortingly.

It was gradually getting dark, but enough light pervaded the coach for Mr. Waterhouse to see his companion clearly. She had ceased to peer from the window, but she was clearly anxious, and found it difficult to keep her hands still in her lap. After a silence of a minute or so, Mr. Waterhouse moved a little nearer to her and said:

"Katharine, there is something I want to tell you." She turned her head and looked at him inquiringly. "You remember I said I had business in Bath? Well, my dear, that business concerns you."

She raised her brows and looked at him in surprise. "Me, sir. What possible business can you have with me?"

"It is the business of restoring

something you have lost, my dear."

She laughed now. "Have I lost something? That is very careless of me, George, but surely there was no need for you to come all the way from London to restore it to me?"

"On the contrary, my dear, there was every reason. You see, *this* is what you lost." His right hand was inside his coat and slowly he drew something from an inside pocket. Even in the dim light she knew what it was, as it lay glistening green and gold. She gave a gasp. "Oh, George! My necklace! How ever did you get it back?" She stared at him, wide-eyed. "Oh, George, did you get it from the thief, for if you did you must tell me who it is for they think Christopher is responsible!"

Mr. Waterhouse gave no answer, but stared into her eyes for a moment, his own strangely brilliant. Then he laughed softly and dropped the necklace into her lap.

She knew, then. For a breathless moment she stared at him, her mouth a little open, as the implications of her knowledge slowly appeared. It was George who was the thief, the murderer. So it must have been George who informed against her husband, who wanted him taken for the crime he did not commit. It had always been George, and now, while seeking to help her husband, she was carrying to him the very man responsible for his plight.

"It's you, isn't it," she said throbbingly, the colour mounting in her cheeks. "It was you who took my necklace and those other things, and you who killed your own accomplice. You planned it from the beginning, didn't you, making Christopher say things to incriminate himself, and now you are planning to finish your business! Oh, it was very neat, I have to admit it. I suppose escorting me to parties and seeming so friendly was just to discover where poor Christopher was hiding."

He made no answer, but a mocking smile lifted his thin upper lip, and he stared down at her with a glint in his eyes.

"But why did you kill that poor man, George? The one who had helped you in all those robberies." She gave a little laugh. "But how silly I am! Of course you had to kill him, for he was the only possible link with you. I suppose Christopher saw you?"

"Yes, he saw me, and was foolish enough to be spotted by the Watch, leaning over the body. He played into my hands."

"Yes, he did, and so did I, by quarrelling with Christopher that night. It made it only too easy for you."

"It did, but I should have done it anyway. There was never any problem with you."

"No," she flashed, "until I nearly recognised you!"

He smiled. "That was an anxious moment, I must admit. You should be glad, however, that you did not, for you are still alive."

"Yes," she agreed bitterly, "but for

how much longer?"

"Oh, I doubt that I shall kill you, my dear. There is not the need. No one will believe your story, the weight of evidence against your poor Christopher is too strong. It will merely look as though you are trying to save him."

"But what of Christopher himself? You will have to kill him, won't you?"

Mr. Waterhouse appeared to consider this. "I must admit, the idea of mutual suicide for you and dear Christopher vastly appeals, but I hope it shall not come to that. If he is sensible he will merely end his days on the hangman's rope."

Katharine managed a laugh. "How simple it all is, to be sure! And I suppose, if I do not 'commit suicide' I shall just fade into obscurity and be forgotten, or remembered only as the wife of that notorious thief and murderer."

"As a matter of fact, my dear, I have other plans for you." He moved a little closer. "I must admit, my aim at first was simply your beautiful necklace. I've wanted it for a long time, you know, even before it became necessary for me to seek other forms of finance. My father lusted after it too, and he used to speak of it, how beautiful it was, when I was small. I waited a long time for it to be brought out of the bank. So I befriended you. But you are brave, my dear. I shall not forget how calm you were that evening when for all you know I could have shot you. I remember thinking as I saw you home that night how truly admirable you were and how wicked it was that you were married to poor Veryan. It made my pursuit of you all the more sweet, and my crushing of your husband all the more determined."

"That I believe! Perhaps you could tell me, sir, just what your plans for me are."

"Certainly, but I am surprised you do not guess. Or perhaps you do." He looked hard at her and she reddened, but said nothing. "I would give you a very good life, you know. I admit, my finances have been a little shaky of late, but I have hopes of soon repairing them. I have been having the most amazing run of luck! And who knows, when you are a widow, I might even be persuaded to marry you!"

"Be careful, sir, how you gamble, lest your luck change!"

He looked amused. "I do not envisage that, my dear. At least, not so long as I am playing such inexpert opposition as dear Veryan!"

Katharine gave an exaggerated sigh. "Well, I suppose I should be grateful. It is not every day one has proposals for marriage before one's first husband is even dead."

Mr. Waterhouse looked at her, a smile curling his lips. "Katharine, my dear, you always seemed such a mouse, but now I know you are truly magnificent!"

"I believe I should be honoured, sir, but indeed, I cannot find it within me to thank you!"

Mr. Waterhouse seemed a little hurt. "I think you might try, however, Katharine, my dear. After all, I have been instrumental in relieving you of the most tiresome husband!"

The grey eyes flashed. "How dare you speak so of Christopher! Even if he were a murderer I would never be persuaded to be so faithless!"

"Admirable sentiments, my dear, I am sure, but don't you think just a little misplaced? Never in his life has Veryan deserved such passion. He is completely worthless, my dear, and the sooner you realize it, the better it will be for all of us!"

"You can say what you like about Christopher, but at least he is honest!"

"*Honest*, my dear?" Mr. Waterhouse seemed amazed at the thought. "Hardly honest, Katharine. Why, he has been having an affair with Lady Sherreden for years, even under your nose!"

Katharine achieved a scornful laugh. "Indeed, sir, you must do better than that! You forget, Lady Sherreden is my sister-in-law, and I know her very well. I also know the full extent of my husband's relationship with her, and whatever she may say, I trust Christopher."

"Then you are a fool, Katharine, and you disappoint me. It seems I must tell you some other truths about your husband."

"You had better try harder, then, sir, if you mean to succeed with me!"

"Very well. Before your wedding with the young Marquis I entered on a wager with him that he would not find anyone fool enough to marry him within a week."

Katharine held her breath and praised the shadow of the chaise. It was something she had had no idea of, and as a blow it was a hard one. Somehow, however, she controlled her breathing, and turned to him with a little smile. "What are you telling me, sir, that my husband enjoys a wager? This is a paltry attempt, I assure you! I have always known why Christopher married me, and there is nothing you can say that will persuade me to shift my loyalties."

"Simply because I killed a man, my dear? Oh, come now, poor reason, that! Why, until a few minutes ago Christopher was a murderer and a thief, and you were prepared to fight for him!"

"Your argument is useless, Mr. Waterhouse. I never believed Christopher to be any of those things, and besides, even if he were, nothing would persuade me to desert him, least of all your poisoned arrows! You see, Mr. Waterhouse, I happen to love him!"

She glared at him defiantly, her bosom heaving, and for a moment Mr. Waterhouse knew an impulse to take her into his arms. "Has it occurred to you, Katharine, that you are quite at my mercy?"

Her laugh was genuine. "Mr. Waterhouse, what novels have you been reading? I have only to call out, you know, for the coachman to come to my assistance."

"They would not hear you, my dear. Both the coachman and the groom have been known to be amazingly deaf on occasions."

For the first time since entering the chaise Katharine knew real fear. There was a holster at her elbow, with a pistol lodged in it, but she had no way of telling whether it was loaded. She pulled it out, however, and pointed it at her captor. "Keep away, Mr. Waterhouse. If you frighten me I shall not hesitate to use it."

The gentleman glanced at the pistol and gave a soft laugh. "Do not be foolish, my dear, it is not loaded. You could do no damage with that."

"You think not? I am not so weak, however. I wonder just how hard I could hit you if I tried?" She put her head on one side and appeared to consider the matter. Mr. Waterhouse laughed and moved away.

"Very well, Katharine, you win this

time. We shall have leisure enough in the future to debate the matter."

A silence ensued. The feeling that Mr. Waterhouse was merely amused by her defiance did not encourage Katharine, and she sat in her corner in mingled anger and apprehension. There was nothing she could do. The horses did not hesitate, there was no chance for Katharine to leap into the road. And even if she had summoned her courage for this daring feat, what then? She could not offer help to her husband by stranding herself in the middle of nowhere, and the knowledge would not quite go away that Mr. Waterhouse no longer had need of her.

It was barely thirteen miles to the address in Bristol, and the horses the Duke had given them were good. The journey was never completed, however. Forty-five minutes after leaving Cheard a halloo from the box announced the fact that a coach was up ahead. Katharine had been sitting thoughtfully in her corner, the pistol nursed in her lap, but at this she started, and peered anxiously through the window. Clouds covered the moon and for a moment all was darkness, then they parted and the road was flooded with a pale light that filtered down through the trees. The rectangle of darkness up ahead was swaying heavily. Although Katharine could catch no sound above the thunder of their own wheels, there was no doubt in her mind that this was Christopher. She sat nervously on the edge of the seat, grasping the pistol tightly, taking comfort in its cold solidity.

The road was narrow at this point. A bank rose steeply away from them on the right, and there were suggestions that the hill fell sharply through the trees on the left. Katharine, peering anxiously forward, began to hope that the carriage would not be stopped, but at that moment a shout above her caused her heart to miss a beat.

"Hey, there! Lord Veryan's chaise! We have her ladyship behind you!"

She knew he would stop. He must stop. Even had he known who else was in the chaise he would have issued the same order. The carriage slowed, and in a moment had come to a halt. Katharine shivered.

At once Mr. Waterhouse became active. He pulled a pearl-handled pistol from his coat, and, throwing open the door, jumped down into the road. The hope that he would forget about her and that she might at last be of help quickly vanished as she heard the hurried order: "Watch her ladyship, Henry. Jacob come with me." A scuffling sound above signified that the coachman and groom were descending, and then a broad face appeared in the open door. Katharine sat still.

The groom had descended also, and now marched purposefully at Mr. Waterhouse's side. The door of the carriage ahead was suddenly thrown open and a figure, dark against the trees, jumped down into the road.

"Cover the coachman, Jacob," said Mr. Waterhouse softly. "Well, Veryan, we meet again in a lonely, unfrequented spot!"

An oath escaped his lordship. "Damn you, George! That's a damned plot if ever I saw one! I suppose I should have guessed."

"I suppose you might, except it so happens her ladyship is here, in my chaise, to be exact."

The scurrying clouds uncovered the moon again and showed his lordship's face to be contorted with rage. "If you've hurt her, Waterhouse — "

"Save your wrath, Veryan. I have not touched her, and shall not, until you are safely dead."

Lord Veryan laughed harshly. "A merry plan, my friend, but perhaps I do not die so easily!"

"Take care, Veryan, do not taunt me. It is not my plan to kill you. I am content to let justice do its work. However, should you wish to fight, I am certain I shall be pardoned for killing such a desperate villain as yourself!"

Lord Veryan's teeth flashed in an angry smile. "You have not won yet, George! I have no mind to let you take me."

"I think my lord forgets! Henry, let our friend have a glimpse of his lady."

There was a scuffling sound from the second coach and the pugilistic Henry Jicks appeared, holding Lady Veryan by the arm. She gave no appearance of struggling.

"You see, Veryan, I still hold the ace! Although I must admit to a certain reluctance to dispose of so lovely a lady, I assure you, my dear Lord Veryan, I shall not hesitate should it prove expedient."

Lord Veryan stood silent. The form of Mr. Jicks was a little comforting, but there was no knowing whether feelings that had once undergone a change might not be easily persuaded to change back. He regarded the pugilist through narrowed lids and relaxed. He had seen the smallest nod.

The pearl-handled pistol glinted a little in the moonlight. "Take me, then, George, if you can!" He became conscious of movement behind him, and in the same instant a jerk in the hand of Mr. Waterhouse. He dived as the pistol exploded, and a bullet scorched his ear. He landed heavily, face-downwards in the road, and rolled quickly to see Mr. Waterhouse bearing down on him. He saw too a third man, mounted, levelling a weapon in his direction. He rolled again.

The road ended abruptly. As a second bullet whizzed past his cheek Lord Veryan felt the ground slip suddenly away, and he was rolling downwards, crashing through under-growth and bushes that scratched his hands and face unmercifully. He was aware of confusion up above, and two more shots sounded, one thudding sharply into a tree as he crashed past it. Several times he grasped at the flailing branches, but succeeded in nothing more than tearing the skin from his already lacerated hands. A dark bush loomed ahead and he hit it hard, putting out his hand at the moment of impact. It did not resist, but his momentum was lessened, and consequently he saw the tree before he hit it. With an effort he bunched his legs under his chin and covered his face with his hands.

13

AT first he thought it was a bee, and tried to shake his head. The noise continued, and as his consciousness returned he knew it was inside his ears. His head felt strangely heavy, and then, as he raised his eyelids, he realized he was hanging almost upside down. There was a throbbing at the top of his nose and behind his eyes. He tried to focus, and for a moment thought his sight had failed since total blackness greeted him, then after a moment he saw something pale and realized it was his hand. The darkness was only night-time. He lay where he was for several more minutes. There was no pain in his body, although his head throbbed unmercifully, and it seemed easiest to lie where he was. In a moment he would remember. Gradually he became aware of feeling in the hand he could see, something rough and damp beneath his fingers. He moved them a little, and interpreted the matter. Decaying leaves, and twigs. A wood, then. What the devil was he doing hanging upside down in a wood? He decided that the first thing he should do was to get himself the right way up. This did not prove easy. He presumed he still had his legs, and that they were attached to the nether end of his body, but it was a matter of faith rather than knowledge, because all feeling ended at his armpits. He lifted the arm he could see, and by throwing it out behind him tried to roll over onto his back. He succeeded, and as he did so, a wracking pain was set up in the region of his ribs, and he knew too that his legs had not deserted him. For a few minutes here he lay still, staring upwards now through the branches to the black and white sky. As he lay, it became apparent to him that a tree rose from almost where he was, and in a moment he realized that this very tree was what was holding him upside down and indeed, preventing him from falling. He seemed to be wrapped round it, his body bent curiously at the waist.

Of a sudden he began remembering; a falling sensation, crashing through bushes and branches, and the sound of a bullet thudding into a tree above him. With these came other recollections, and a burning sensation in his right ear obtruded itself on his notice. A picture presented itself: George, whom he hated, with a pistol; two men, one on a horse, shooting at him, the other with his arm round his wife. Protecting her? No. Threatening her, but for some reason the threat was not to be worried about.

He remembered it all, then. Stretching out his left hand he found the roughened bark of the tree that had stopped him. Gradually he pushed himself into a sitting position and leaned back gratefully against the trunk. The feeling had long since returned to his limbs, and although they seemed to hurt down their length, the pain was entirely superficial, deriving solely from a multitude of scratches, bruises, and abrasions.

He had no idea how long he had lain there, but the wood seemed totally silent. There was none of those sounds that might be associated with an extensive search — men breaking through the undergrowth, an occasional exchange of shouts. Time, then, had definitely elapsed. He had sat against the tree for several minutes before he realized that the pain in his head was not going to stop, and that he could not remain where he was. There was George to find. Instinctively his hand went for his sword hilt, and it was with a chill in his breast that he discovered it was missing. His belt, too, was gone. It must have been torn off in his fall.

For another minute he strained his ears. The wood was silent of all noises except those that could be expected. An owl called, and a mouse rustled in the leaves behind him. All else was silent. With an effort Lord Veryan came to his feet. He could not meet Mr. Waterhouse unarmed, and his pistols lay snug in their black case in his chaise. If his fall had been straight, there was a chance his sword might be retrieved. It was all he could hope.

Carefully, therefore, and trying to make no more noise than he need, he left the security of the oak and began the steep ascent. He had no idea how far he had fallen but he knew perfectly well that however far it was it would seem a lot further going back. The intermittent clouds made the going slow, for the moon was often covered, and then barely any light filtered through the branches to the ground beneath. He became acutely aware of all his cuts and grazes, and the throbbing in his head made all movement painful. Bushes leapt up to scratch and tear him whenever he was unwary, and the frequent darkness made his search for his sword almost impossible. There was no sign of the road above him. The trees stretched interminably upwards until he began to wonder if he had fallen off this earth. There was no sound among the trees save that of his own feet as he kicked away the dried and rotting leaves. He found his sword by stepping on it. The metal was hard and painful beneath his feet, and as he looked down a shaft of moonlight glittered on the hilt. With a feeling of intense relief he caught it up. The belt was still attached and he was just about to put it on when he realized how very light the whole thing was he looked at it, then, the sound of his own heart deafening in his ears. The blade was broken off short. Less than six inches extended beneath the hilt.

For a moment his brain was paralyzed. He had put all his hopes on the recovery of the weapon, and now it lay broken and useless in his hands. With an effort he cast his mind ahead. There was no help for it. He must find his chaise and the pistols within it. As he cast the broken sword away, however, another thought occurred to him, and he scanned the ground quickly. The blade of his sword lay there, still in the torn remnants of the scabbard. He picked it up, and thoughtfully drew forth the short blade. An excellent dagger, if only it had a handle. He stared at it hard for several minutes, then retrieved the discarded hilt and belt. The blade nearest the hilt was not the sharpest part, but he set to cutting six inches off the bottom of the leather scabbard. The leather was tough and the blade blunt, but Lord Veryan was determined, and channelled his strength into the futile exercise. He tore the end away at last, and slipped the broken blade back into its sheath. Six inches of blade protruded, sharp and shining, from the end. And he had a guard to hold it with. Just having something to grasp lightened the load on the Marquis's shoulders, and he plunged forward with renewed courage in search of his pistols.

He gained the road in time. The trees suddenly grew thin before him, and the pale light lit up the clearing of the road. He held his breath then, and, clutching the remains of his sword firmly, he stepped silently onto the road. He had come out to the right of the chaises, both of which were still stationed in the road. He thought at first that they were deserted, but as he moved forward slowly in the cover of the trees a man appeared from the woods and stopped beside Lord Veryan's chaise. Another man came from the shadows, and the two stood talking for a while. Then the first man nodded, and set off down the road.

Lord Veryan stood a while in the darkness, watching the remaining man stamping his feet and blowing into his hands. He seemed to be some sort of guard, but over what Lord Veryan could not tell. There was no sound except the scrunch and scrape of feet on the road. He began moving forward again, clutching his make-shift dagger for reassurance. The grass at the side of the road deadened all sound, and he gained the shadow of the coach unseen. The guard was now slapping his arms against his chest and interspersing his stamping with little jumps. He was not looking towards the Marquis.

Lord Veryan leant for a moment against the back of the chaise. A guard meant prisoners, and with luck Katharine might still be here. He was almost certain Mr. Waterhouse was not, since he had not appeared when the searcher had returned for instructions. The plan he formulated as he stood there was simple and obvious. He had no mind to kill the guard, and crouching low, felt on the road with his fingers. A rock, hand-sized, was soon discovered, and he stood up again. It was so easy he almost laughed. Tossing it forward, it crashed through the bushes, and rolled noisily down the bank until brought to a stop by some obstacle. The guard reacted predictably. Carefully he drew forth his pistol, and approached the woods. It would take him several minutes, the Marquis thought, to search the area thoroughly. He gave him a few minutes to be out of sight, then rounded the side of the chaise and carefully opened the door. There were two dark bundles inside, one on the floor, one heaped onto the seat. A pair of eyes regarded him beseechingly, and the Marquis had to stifle a laugh.

"Hello, Joseph! At least you're alive!" He stepped inside, carefully closing the door behind him. The bundle on the floor proved to be his groom, tied so that he was quite helpless. With a heave Lord Veryan pulled him up and sat him on the seat. Then with a grin he pulled down the mufflers that had so effectively gagged them.

"God bless you, my lord!" said Joseph, feelingly. "I thought I would stifle behind that smelly thing!"

Lord Veryan disregarded this. "Where's my wife, Joseph? In the other carriage?"

Joseph shook his head despondently.

"No, my lord. He took her up the hill to some barn he found. Said it would be safer for her. Overheard him, like; hardly surprising, the way he was shouting it about. I've a mind he didn't mean you to get her away easy-like."

"No, I see that. Tell me, Joseph, how long ago was this? I've been lying in the woods for goodness knows how long."

Joseph considered. "Well, it seems an age, my lord, but I suppose it can't be above three hours. The moon's pretty high now. I doubt if it's yet midnight."

Lord Veryan nodded thoughtfully. "Tell me, Joseph, which direction is this barn?"

Joseph, whose hands were still tied, nodded his head up the hill. "Took her straight up, almost, he did. Can't be far, though, because it never took him above ten minutes to find it."

"Thank you, Joseph, you're a good man. I suppose they found my pistols?"

Joseph's teeth flashed in the moonlight. "God bless you, my lord, I kept them safe. I had thought I might use them, saving I couldn't use my hands to load them." With an effort he inched along the seat, revealing the slim box. "They threw me in on top of it, see. Took the pistols from the holsters, but never thought to look for these."

Lord Veryan grinned. "Probably thought I would never be fool enough to leave them! Thank you, Joseph, I won't forget. Now, if you'll forgive me, I'll just muffle you up again."

"Aren't you taking us with you, my lord? Three's more use than one." His voice almost pleaded for his freedom.

Lord Veryan smiled, but shook his head. "If I let you free, Joseph, they'll know I've been back, then they'll all be after me. I'd rather face Mr. Waterhouse alone, if you don't mind. Be on the watch for the one with a squashed face. He is supposed to be for us, although I sometimes wonder about him."

"Old Henry?" Joseph sounded

scornful. "He threw us in here like so much straw!"

Lord Veryan frowned. "Well, it can't be helped. He might be playing his own game. We must wait and find out." With that, he carefully muffled up his servants, and, after a moment's thought, dropped his make-shift dagger on the seat. "You might find it useful! Take care!" Joseph's eyes showed resignation and Lord Veryan, grinning, jumped out of the chaise.

He was not too soon. The guard, having scanned as much of wood as he thought necessary, decided to check his prisoners. Lord Veryan had barely pushed the door closed before the opposite one opened and the guard peered inside. Apparently satisfied, he shut the door again and in a moment had relaxed against it.

Crouching low against the opposite side of the chaise Lord Veryan considered his position. The barn must be his objective, but a stretch of road lay between him and the opposite bank, and the decoy trick would not work a second time on a guard whose senses were no doubt very much on the alert. His pistols lay in his lap, but they were not loaded, and could not be safely by the light of the moon. The lamps on the chaise were still flickering dimly, and he decided, therefore, that his pistols must be loaded and ready before he left that spot.

Lord Veryan was an expert shot. He had been loading pistols since his childhood when, unbeknownst to his parents, his cousin Edward had given him a pistol to play with, and had shown him how to load it and fire it. Had he been asked, he would have said he could load it with his eyes shut, but now that his trial came, he found it no easy task. The light afforded by the lamps was unsteady, and resulted in some powder spillage. It was done at last, however, and Lord Veryan, having pushed the lined black box out of sight under the chaise, hastily pocketed one pistol on each side of his coat.

A cautious glance satisfied him that the guard was no longer as alert as he had been. He was lolling at his ease against the side of the coach, and, as Lord Veryan watched, drew a cigar from an inner pocket and lit it, striking the match carelessly against the side of the coach. The light flared briefly, showing the contours of the man's face, then it died, and was tossed into the bushes.

Barely ten feet of road lay between Lord Veryan and the cover of the other side, but the road was stony and rough, and there was no tuft of grass to soften his footsteps. Cautiously, therefore, he started across the road, walking as slowly as his nerve would let him, waiting always for the crunch that would betray him. The ten feet seemed to stretch into a hundred, but at last the grass was beneath his feet once more, and the guard had not been alerted.

The hill stretched up and away into the darkness. A line of trees flanked the road a few feet away, but beyond that, as far as he could see, was open pasture or common land. No building or barn was apparent, but he knew the general direction and started off up the hill. The going was almost as difficult as it had been to cross the wood. The light from the moon was intermittent, and several times tussocks rose up to catch his feet or rabbit holes dropped away before him. Once a solitary hawthorn loomed without warning and he was in it before he realized, scratching his face and hands painfully. The urge to rush on was almost overwhelming. The thought of Katharine helpless with George was unbearable, and he thought that, if anything happened to her, he would not care what George did to him. His vision was frequently marred by the idea of Katharine's face, and the funny sideways look she would give him, from beneath her lashes, that always gave him a strange, constricted feeling in his throat. With an effort he attempted to banish the thought, and concentrate on the matter in hand. He was forced to stop for several minutes while a particularly large and thick cloud obscured the moon completely, then, when the ground was once more illuminated, stumbled on towards the top of the hill. As he neared the brow a hunched shape suddenly appeared silhouetted against the sky-line, and moved slowly towards him. For a moment Lord Veryan froze, his fingers closing round the comforting shape of the pistol in his pocket, then he relaxed, and almost laughed. The sheep passed harmlessly by.

The top of the hill afforded a view of a deep valley, wooded on one side, with a solitary farmhouse nestling beside a stream. He hesitated for a moment, wondering whether the building beneath him was the one George had referred to, decided that it was not and cast around for an alternative.

On his left the crest of the hill rose upwards to another peak and here, the roof outline just visible against the deep blue of the night sky, was another building. As he stared, he thought he caught the flicker of a flame somewhere inside, and at once turned towards it. He had to move cautiously. There was always the possibility that George was waiting for him, standing at the window and watching his every move. He decided to make a wide circle around the barn and come on it from behind where the slope of the hill would afford him advantage. He plotted the course by the moonlight, then waited, and when cloud once more made all dark started off on his projected route. Progress was slow; he was moving almost blindly and bent himself double lest in an incautious moment his figure be outlined against the sky and reveal him to his enemy. He arrived eventually, however, and stood looking down on the barn. There were two doors, one large and double, the other a small, single door at one end. Above, high up on the wall, was a square opening over which a large metal hook was sunk deep into the wall. As he watched the wind rose slightly, and caught upon something that depended from the hook, making it swing gently against the wall. Cautiously he approached the building. It was as he had thought. A rope, used for hauling bundles of straw, had been left on the hook, and afforded him a method of entry. Just how he would climb the rope he was uncertain, but he supposed it might be achieved by clasping the rope and walking up the wall. In the event it proved harder than he had imagined. The rope cut into his already sore hands, and it was no easy business to move his hands one above the other without sliding to the bottom. Then it must all be done silently. The slightest scuffle of his boots on the wall would alert those inside, and his only hope depended on coming on Mr. Waterhouse unawares.

The moment his foot touched the wide ledge was perhaps one of the most relieved of his life. Carefully he transferred his weight from his hands to his feet and thankfully released the rope. Rubbing his chaffed hands, he peered down into the barn.

He was high above the ground. Far beneath him, a lantern stood on the floor, casting a flickering and inadequate light around the barn. Beside it on the floor sat Katharine, bound hand and foot, an expression of acute anguish on her face. An enormous mound of straw was heaped against the side of the wall, and Lord Veryan, his eyes fixed on his wife's slim figure, stepped hastily onto the top of the pile, his feet sinking deep into the straw. Katharine's expression gave him the warning, but it came too late. A voice, smooth and mocking, sounded above him, and caused him to freeze where he stood.

"So, my lord, at last you are here! I confess I expected you a while ago, but I suppose it is of little consequence. What became of you in that wood?"

Slowly Lord Veryan turned. Crouched above him, his sword balanced delicately in one hand, was Mr. Waterhouse, a smile on his thin lips.

"A tree hit me," Lord Veryan explained shortly.

Mr. Waterhouse clicked his tongue sympathetically. "I am sorry, Veryan. However, you found the rope alright, I see, so your brain cannot have been too badly affected. Now, shall we join the fair Lady Veryan?" Standing up, Mr. Waterhouse brought the blade to rest lightly against Lord Veryan's shoulder-blade and the two of them descended to ground level. Katharine looked up at him anxiously.

"I'm sorry, Christopher, truly I am, but he said he'd shoot you if I warned you."

"Don't worry. I have no reason to doubt his word. At least I'm alive."

"Yes, but I'm so worried about what will happen now. You must think me dreadful, not wanting to see you, but — "

"I suppose," Mr. Waterhouse interrupted smoothly, "that I should leave you two alone, as you have not seen each other for so long, but I must admit I am not of a mind to do so. You see, Ver, there's no knowing what you might get up to if I left you to yourselves. So I'm afraid there is but one answer. Your pistols, Ver, and your sword."

"I have no sword," the Marquis replied shortly.

Mr. Waterhouse laughed. "Now, Veryan do you expect me to believe you would come out unarmed? Really, you must think me very foolish!"

Lord Veryan shrugged and said nothing. Growing impatient, Mr. Waterhouse thrust his captive into the light of the lantern and there, to his surprise, discovered the truth of his lordship's statement. His eyebrows rose, then he laughed softly.

"Pistols you certainly have!" Swiftly

he plunged a hand into each pocket, keeping sword point against the Marquis's throat. Both weapons went into his own pocket. "And now I'm afraid I must leave you, both of you. My lord, if you would care to sit by your wife, I shall bind you, unpleasant, but I fear necessary. I think you had better comply, my lord, before I spear your lovely wife." Lord Veryan, who had looked highly reluctant, glanced briefly at his wife, whose grey eyes were huge and apprehensive, and silently seated himself beside her. Mr. Waterhouse chuckled, and rapidly wound a length of rope about Lord Veryan's wrists, his arms pulled tightly across his back. Then, without cutting the rope, he stretched it to Lord Veryan's ankles, giving him a kick so that he rolled over onto his stomach. Then his ankles too were tied, his legs bent at the knees, so that he was completely helpless.

Satisfied at last, Mr. Waterhouse stood up, and carefully removed several pieces of straw from his breeches. "My dear Katharine, I really regret the necessity of this. Had you not been so rebellious we might have come to some arrangement, but, I fear me, a reluctant bride would be the very devil. I hope you will not regret your decision." He sighed and shook his head. "Well, my friends, in a moment I must leave you. There is just time, ah, to prepare my defence. One must be so careful, you know, when dealing with hardened criminals."

"Mr. Waterhouse," said Katharine suddenly, "what are you going to do?"

"A funeral pyre, my dear. A fitting end, do you not think? The loving wife dying at the side of her faithless husband! A sad accident with a lantern. But first, as I said, my security." So saying he caught up the oil lamp and removed the glass cover, exposing the feeble flame. Then to Katharine's horror, he held his left arm over the flame until the fine cloth caught and smouldered. The lamp being set down, the three of them watched as the flame licked up his arm and Mr. Waterhouse drew in his breath sharply as the burning cloth fell away and exposed the skin. Then, stripping off his coat he hurriedly beat out the flames until just a thin column of smoke rose from the charred material. Despite the greyish tinge to his lips, Mr. Waterhouse smiled, and carefully returned his rapidly blistering arm to the coat.

"I salute you, George," said Lord Veryan dryly. "A sad accident, as you say. No doubt you tried to save us, even at your peril, but were unfortunately driven back by the strength of the flames."

Mr. Waterhouse laughed softly. "As you say, my lord, a sad and tragic accident! And now, my friends, the finale!" The lamp was caught up, Mr. Waterhouse swung back his arm and hurled it into the corner of the barn where it instantly smashed, spilling oil onto the straw beneath. At once flames leapt up the wall, rapidly catching the dry straw and setting up a merry crackling. Mr. Waterhouse paused only to see the fire well caught, then he opened the door and vanished into the darkness.

14

"**W**HERE the devil's Freddie?" exclaimed Lord Veryan, struggling against the ropes that bound him.

Katharine, who was trying in vain to loosen her wrists, paused a moment to glance at her husband. "Freddie? Is he coming, then?"

"My God, I hope so! He was on his way to Bow Street when I left him. Mind you, the Duke might have dissuaded him for reasons of his own."

Katharine looked anguished. "Oh dear! My fault, too! Christopher, I am sorry about not seeing you today. I — "

"Don't say anything, Katty. If we get out of this, and at the moment it seems unlikely, I'll make it up to you, I promise. My God, I certainly need to."

Katharine hesitated. "Christopher — "

"Katty, the ropes!"

"Oh yes." Katharine, thus admonished, concentrated on the task in hand.

The barn was rapidly growing hot. The fire now covered one side of the barn and was swiftly creeping towards the pile of straw at their backs. Lord Veryan, who had been straining against his bonds, suddenly relaxed. "It's no good, I can't do it. Katty, can you stand? I can't."

With an effort Katharine heaved herself into a kneeling position, then, getting purchase on the floor with her toes, rocked backwards and onto her feet. She nearly fell over at once, since her skirt had caught beneath her boot, but she stumbled, and regained her balance.

"Good girl! Now, do you think you can get a handful of burning straw?"

"Burning straw! Christopher — !"

"Katharine, the only way we can get out of this inferno is for you to burn away the rope that joins my feet to my hands! You must, or we shall be burned alive! Don't you understand?"

Katharine looked at him for a second, and then started to jump across the uneven floor towards the flames. She did not have far to go. The flames were creeping nearer all the time. Crouching low, and peering over her shoulder at her bound hands, Katharine clasped a bunch of straw between her numbed fingers and carefully applied it to the blaze. It caught at once, and Lord Veryan, seeing the straw flare in his wife's hands, rolled across the floor to meet her. As Katharine knelt with her back to his the flames licked Lord Veryan's bare hands, but beyond biting his lip he gave no sign. Pulling the rope taut between his hands and feet he felt the fibres slacken, then, as Katharine dropped the remnants of her straw torch with a little cry of pain, a final wrench completed his freedom.

There was little time to spare. As Lord Veryan's cut and blistered fingers fumbled with the knots that bound his wife, the flames reached their feet and they took rapid steps backwards. The knots about Katharine's feet were pulled hard with her straining, but Lord Veryan's frantic fumblings finally released her and they looked about for their escape. The flames had reached the roof of the barn, and all the straw that had been piled up against one wall was ablaze. One of the main beams was beginning to smoulder, and the large double doors had also caught. There seemed no way out. The other door had long since been smothered, and the window through which Lord Veryan had made his entry was now quite inaccessible. The double doors, which lay across a sea of flames, were their only hope. A glance at Katharine's long skirt made Lord Veryan's heart sink. He made a quick decision.

"Katharine, get on my back. *Quickly!* Hitch up your skirts, for God's sake, and hang on tight!"

She made no demur. Ladylike behaviour was not considered. Lifting her skirts above her knees she clambered onto her husband's back, and wound one arm round his neck and the other beneath his right arm.

"Good girl! Now, whatever you do, don't let go!" He gave her no chance to protest. The flames before them were several feet high, and the enormous wooden door was burning at the bottom. He took a breath, then plunged shoulder first towards the door. The momentum carried him into it, and with a kick he had thrust it open. They fell out onto the grass just as a beam feel from the roof and the barn became impassable. Katharine's skirts were caught, and Lord Veryan, dragging off his own charred coat, smothered them as she lay crying on the grass.

"Katharine, are you burned? Katharine!"

She sniffed, gave a hiccuping sob, and allowed herself to be helped into a sitting position. She gave a watery smile. "Well, my lord, you are a surprise! I had never thought you to be a hero!"

"Neither had I! To tell the truth, I felt very much inclined just to give up at one point, but then I couldn't really let George get away with everything, could I?"

Katharine smiled at him.

"But tell me, are you hurt?"

"My fingers got a bit burned from holding that straw, and of course my dress is quite ruined, but otherwise I'm alright. But what about you?"

He held up his coat and smiled ruefully. The tails were still smouldering and a large hole had been burned through the front panel. "We were lucky. Another minute and we would have been inside *that*. Come on." He helped her to her feet and they started down the hill, their way lit by the flames that leapt high above the barn. A crashing sound made them halt, and as they looked back the remains of the roof fell through into the blaze beneath. Katharine shut her eyes for a moment, then they turned and continued down the hill.

Their progress was far easier than the assent had been. For several hundred yards beyond the fire it was as light as day. As they approached the road, however, Lord Veryan laid a hand on his wife's arm in warning. A third chaise stood before them and several men were conversing in the centre of the road.

"Really, sir, I must ask you to cease these accusations! They do you no good, and I should not blame Mr. Waterhouse if he found himself a great deal provoked, especially after the shock he has just suffered!"

"When are you going to listen to me?" exclaimed an exasperated Mr. Malling. "This is your man here, and if Lord and Lady Veryan have had an accident in a barn then I know perfectly well who is responsible!"

"Mr. Malling, sir, what you say is very serious! I must ask you to desist!"

"Really, Freddie," came the voice of Mr. Waterhouse, plainly tried, "how many times must I tell you? He struggled with me and knocked over the lamp. I tried to save him, I was even burned myself, but it was quite useless. Lady Veryan, too. She refused to believe he could not be saved." There was a short silence. "Now, Seel, if you please, I shall be on my way. This business has been prolonged enough."

"Come on, Katty," whispered his lordship, "this is where we resurrect ourselves." Grasping his wife's hand he jumped down into the road, pulling her after him. The noise caused heads to turn, and for a moment there was total silence. Then Mr. Malling, relief blatant on his round, good-humoured countenance, started towards them his arms outstretched.

"My God, Ver, you don't know how happy you've just made me! Come and listen to the lies this fellow is talking!"

Mr. Waterhouse, who had gone even

greyer, attempted a recover . "So you escaped, both of you, and not much hurt, by the look of you! I'm only sorry I wasn't of more help. However, I'm afraid escaping has not done you much good. Mr. Seel, here, is a Runner."

"Yes, George, I know. Good evening, gentlemen, I have been expecting you some little time. Had you arrived earlier we might have been saved a great deal of discomfiture."

Mr. Malling grinned ruefully. "Yes, well, I'm sorry about that, Ver, but it took me a devil of a time to persuade these fellows to come at all! Kept on saying some other cove had already left with two of their fellows! Rum thing. Couldn't understand it at all. Then that plaguey grandfather of yours, Ver, wouldn't tell us where you were! Thought he was protecting you, or some such thing! Cursed nuisance! However, we're here now."

"That's alright, Freddie. Now I think we had better settle this business finally. Mr. Jicks! Are you here?"

The broad form of the one-time pugilist emerged from behind Mr. Waterhouse's chaise. "Yes, guv-nor, I'm 'ere, an' ready an' all."

"So there's that fellow!" exclaimed Mr. Malling. "Where the devil have you been hiding yourself? I had these fellows here thinking me a dashed liar!"

Mr. Jicks rubbed his nose. "Ay, well, I'm sorry about that, guv-nor, but it seemed best, at the time, with Mr. Waterrouse, here, saying them was dead."

The larger of the two Runners began to show impatience. "Lord Veryan, just what is this about? It won't do you good, you know, to procrastinate."

"Well, Mr. Seel, I am hoping Henry here will exonerate me. He has been in my employ some weeks, working so to speak, in the enemy camp."

There came a soft laugh. "Really, Veryan, what is this nonsense? Jicks is my coachman!"

Lord Veryan turned his eyes on Mr.

Waterhouse. "Precisely, George."

"Mr. Jicks," said Seel, whose patience was wearing thin, "just what have you to say?"

The pugilist eyed him thoughtfully. "Simple, guvnor. Mr. Waterhouse, 'ere, my one-time employer, stole them jewels an' dumped Davis. Sure as I'm standing 'ere."

A peculiar choking sound came from Mr. Waterhouse. He took a step backwards, and produced a pistol in each hand. Lord Veryan recognised them as his own. "Keep back, my friends! I shall not scruple to use them, I assure you! I have no desire to swing!"

"Steady on, there, sir," said Seel, inching forward. "Don't do anything unwise. It won't do you a bit of good, I can assure you!"

"What harm can it do? You forget, my man, that you are looking at someone with nothing to lose! Just keep away!" He had been walking backwards all the time, and now came up beside the horse that his man, Joshua, had used, which was still tethered to the Marquis's chaise. "Do not try to follow me! I warn you, I shall not hesitate!" Thrusting one pistol into his pocket, but keeping the other levelled, he swung himself into the rough saddle and gathered up the reins. There was a soft laugh, and he pulled on the horse's mouth. At the same moment there came a muffled curse and Rycart, the second Runner, lurched forward towards the horse. Mr. Waterhouse's hand jerked, there was a loud rapport, and Rycart crumpled on the ground. In the combined light of the blaze and the coach lamps Seel's face rapidly acquired a purple hue and he stepped forward purposefully. Mr. Waterhouse had already extracted the second fire-arm and now aimed with precision at Mr. Seel's bald head. Mr. Malling exclaimed in horror, but at the same moment there was a strange thudding sound. Mr. Waterhouse gave a weird cough; his eyes opened very wide and an expression of acute astonishment spread over his face. Then he plunged forward across the horse's neck. Lord Veryan's broken sword, still with the torn protecting sheath, was embedded between Mr. Waterhouse's shoulder-blades. Horror-struck, they watched helplessly as he slid from the animal to lie in a heap on the road.

"My God!" exclaimed Mr. Malling hoarsely, as Mr. Seel bent over the body. "Whatever happened?"

"It was me, sir." Lord Veryan's coachman, Joseph, appeared on the roof of the chaise, and dropped lightly into the road. "I suppose he's dead?" he inquired conversationally.

Seel stood up and wiped his hands purposefully on his breeches. "Oh ay, he's dead alright, I'm obliged."

"It was not what I intended when I freed myself, sir," said the coachman, stolidly, "but it seemed the best thing at the time."

Seel nodded. "I don't think there'll

be any trouble when I make out my report. Poor Rycart would certainly never 'ave minded."

Lord Veryan came to stare at the crumpled form that was Mr. Waterhouse. "I suppose I ought to feel sad, but for the life of me I'm not! It was a good thing you were there, Joseph."

"Ay, my lord, as long as it don't go rough with me now."

Seel scowled at him. "I told you, dint I? I don't 'old with killing meself, but he was the most desperate criminal I've ever met with in all my days. I don't doubt someone will be grateful to you for saving them a job."

"I suppose we're free to go now, are we, Seel?" asked Lord Veryan. "My wife is exhausted."

"Very well, my lord. Just tell me where you may be found, in case you're needed."

They were disturbed. A coach, lumbering round the corner, had come on them unawares, and now formed a fourth in the line of vehicles blocking the road. A man, stocky and wearing buff breeches, jumped down into the road and approached the little party. He scanned them briefly, ignoring the bodies in the road, and fastened his eye on Lord Veryan.

"I presume you are his lordship, the Marquis of Veryan? Then I must ask you to accompany me back to Bow Street. There is a little matter of murder and three robberies to be accounted for."

★ ★ ★

It was nearly an hour later that the last carriage moved away from that position on the Bath to Bristol road. The newly arrived Runners had taken a little convincing that the Lord Veryan for whom they had come in search was indeed innocent of the charges laid against him, and that the real villain lay on the ground with a broken sword in his back. The unfortunate

Mr. Wick had had a trying day. Not only had he been overturned in a carriage, but when he had finally arrived at the villain's supposed hiding place, it had taken a considerable bribe to elicit the information from one of the Duke's ostlers that the Marquis had taken the Bath road. So it had taken Mr. Seel's personal assurance that Joseph would not abscond from Lord Veryan's employ before the matter of Mr. Waterhouse's death could be reported to the Authorities to persuade the zealous Mr. Wick to let the various parties depart. Consequently it was a weary and rather sore Lord Veryan who climbed into the carriage beside his sleeping wife.

He looked at her for a moment and smiled. The moonlight fell on her face and revealed her to be in completely untroubled slumber, with her hair falling about her shoulders and a sooty smudge on her chin. Her dress had fared badly in the fire, being charred almost to the knee and scorched in other places as well. Deciding not to wake her Lord Veryan seated himself opposite with his back to the horses and watched her in silence. But the jolt of the carriage as it started caused her head to jerk forward and she opened her eyes with a start. The first thing she saw was her husband, grinning cheerfully from across the coach. She returned the smile, and for a moment seemed to have no recollection of preceding events. Then her eyes widened and an anxious look succeeded the smile. She sat up and regarded her husband keenly.

"Is everything alright? You persuaded that horrid little man that you hadn't done anything wrong?"

"Yes, I persuaded him, but I rather think he might give Joseph a difficult time."

"Oh, I do hope not! Surely that nice Mr. Seel will speak for him."

"I hope so. The trouble with Mr. Wick is that he had come a long way, my love, in search of a villain, and to return home without one is something of an anticlimax. What's more, he had to put up with the company of my tedious cousin Edward." He grew thoughtful suddenly. "I wonder what happened to him?"

Katharine laughed. "He wasn't there, was he? Perhaps they disposed of him in some inn."

"An excellent scheme, but I doubt very much if it happened that way. No doubt we shall find him at Cheard."

"Oh." The thought brought no pleasure. "I was hoping I would not have to see him. To think that I might actually have to be civil to someone who betrayed you to the Authorities!"

Lord Veryan laughed and moved to sit beside her. "My poor cousin Edward! How disappointed he will be when I return quite free! I'll wager that at this very moment he is revelling in the thought that it all might be his one day."

"And to think that if anything happens to you it *will* be his! I do hope he doesn't try to dispose of you, Christopher." She looked at him anxiously.

"I wouldn't worry too much about that, Katty," he said, pulling one curl affectionately. "There is a very simple way to ruin any plans of his that follow those lines."

She looked up at him inquiringly.

He laughed and put an arm around her. "What, my little innocent, do you not know? We must have an heir, of course!"

The coach was dark but she put her head down and he knew she was blushing. Biting his lip he withdrew his arm and turned to look out of the window. "There's no hurry, of course, and I shall understand if you find the prospect quite unbearable. But I do hope, Katharine," he turned to her again, "that you might feel some affection for me in time."

She raised her head now and stared at him hard, trying to make out his expression in the darkness. Then she turned away, her brain furiously trying to work out the implications of this remark.

Lord Veryan misunderstood her and sighed. "I know you must be thinking of Elizabeth, and I know how it must seem. The thing is, Katty, there's something I have to tell you. No please," she had made a slight sound, "don't interrupt me. For some little while Elizabeth was my mistress. I won't deny it, and I admit too that we had a lot of fun together. Well, Edward told the Duke, you can guess why, and he gave me the ultimatum — get married and finish with Elizabeth, or he would leave all of the Estate that was unentailed to Edward. I was in pretty deep water at the time, and the prospect of Edward getting all that should be mine certainly rankled. Besides, I knew my grandfather had a perfect right to be angry. So I agreed, and came back to London determined to be married as soon as possible. I saw Elizabeth, and told her my decision. Well, you know Lizzy. As soon as she realized I was proposing to leave her she threw a tantrum. She grew hurt and put on her suffering damsel expression. Then she came up with what she clearly thought was an excellent plan — that I should marry you, and thus have an excuse for continuing to see Elizabeth. I know how it sounds, Katty, but I refused even to consider such a thing. Truly I did. I left Elizabeth then, meaning never to see her again.

"But I'm afraid this isn't all. The next morning I was at my club and somehow or other they were all talking about marriage. Well, it turned out that . . . that George bet me that I could not find a woman . . . foolish enough to marry me without knowing me. He said my prospects were so bad that I could not possibly win the wager. Well, I accepted it. There was some animosity between George and me even then, I'm afraid. However, he gave me one week to be married. Well you can imagine how I found myself. The sum was an improbably high one, too. And besides all that, I had no desire to lose face before George. So I cast about for a suitable partner and I'm afraid you were the only eligible candidate."

There was a short silence. "I know all this."

Lord Veryan's jaw dropped. "You know? But that's impossible! I mean, how can you know?"

She raised her eyes to his. "George told me. He thought it would make me leave you, you see, but I fear he had mistaken me."

"Good God!" said Lord Veryan blankly.

Katharine gave a little laugh. "And as for all that about Elizabeth, well, I worked that out weeks ago, although I have to admit that until I knew about the wager I still had some doubts about your motives."

"The wager made you feel better about it?" He sounded appalled.

"Yes indeed! Oh, not at first, but I soon realized that it was much better for you to have married me just for money than to be near Elizabeth. After all, we all need money," she added practically.

"Good God!" exclaimed Lord Veryan again. He took a breath. "Katharine, I know I have behaved very badly, but if you'll only stay, I promise things will be better." He paused. "I love you, you know. And if you think that one day you could come to feel some affection for me, well — " He stopped, and looked out of the window.

"But Christopher, you idiot! You really mean you don't know?" And she went into a peal of laughter.

He turned to her, astonished. "Katharine! Whatever's the matter?"

She looked at him, and laughed again. "Why you fool! I loved you so much that when you proposed to me I very nearly didn't accept!"

"You mean, you almost *refused* me? Whatever for?"

She smiled. "Well, I knew perfectly well that whatever you were marrying me for it wasn't love, and the thought of actually living with someone who regarded me simply as another acquisition was, well, almost unbearable."

"But you managed to overcome this repulsion." Lord Veryan did not sound very flattered.

"Well, you know, my life with Elizabeth and Robert wasn't exactly rosy, and quite honestly I decided that life with you could not possibly be so bad!" Lord Veryan preserved his silence and Katharine's lips twitched. "You don't seem very pleased," she remarked.

He gave a little laugh. "Well, it certainly doesn't improve my opinion of myself!"

"But Christopher! I thought you knew all this! At least, I thought you knew I was marrying you to escape from Robert and Elizabeth!"

"I suppose I did, but to think that you almost decided marriage with me would be worse than staying where you were!"

"Christopher, you goose! Don't you see? Loving you, as I did, made living with you when you couldn't care a fig for me so much the harder!"

He smiled now, and put his arm round his wife's shoulders. "My poor love! How selfish I must have seemed! But can you love me now?"

She opened her eyes wide. "I hope, my lord, that you do not expect me to leave you!"

"You did once, remember."

She looked subdued. "Yes, I did. You're quite right. But you must admit, it looked so odd when you went away, and then I found you were in Grosvenor Street." A thought struck her. "Christopher, just why were you in Grosvenor Street?"

He gave a little laugh. "I went there to ask Elizabeth to tell you the truth about us. Freddie made me hide from George for fear he would do me an injury after I saw him murder that man — "

"So that's how your hat and cane

were found by the body!"

"Don't interrupt, Katharine."

"Sorry."

"As I say, Freddie made me go to Kensington, of all places. Why he picked such a cursed out of the way place I've no idea, but that's neither here nor there. I can tell you, Katty, the idea of hiding from George seemed preposterous, but I suppose it wasn't, after all."

"No, indeed!" replied his wife warmly. "You saw how easily he killed that poor Mr. Rycart. Why, he would never have scrupled to shoot you, especially since you could send him to the gallows!"

Lord Veryan sighed. "Poor George. You know, Katty, I can't help feeling sorry for the fellow. So clever, too. I suppose he was quite rolled up. I'm glad he never had to hang."

Katharine gave a shudder, and nestled a little closer to her husband. They had passed several minutes in silence when Lord Veryan suddenly said: "Katharine, about that heir — "

She looked up at him, and smiled. Lord Veryan, finding actions easier than words in such a situation, casually placed his other arm about his wife's slim person, and responded unequivocally to the invitation of her up-turned lips.

15

THE door opened. His Grace the Duke of Clayre, seated in a deep, winged chair at a distance from the fire, raised his head, and regarded the servant from beneath his shaggy white brows.

"So, John, they are back."

"Yes, your Grace," responded John, bowing stiffly. "I have taken the liberty of putting his lordship in the chamber adjoining Lady Veryan's your Grace. It seems Lord Peter's apartment, which I had prepared, is quite unsuitable."

The old man's brilliant eyes twinkled. "It is, eh? The young dog! No trouble for 'em, then?"

"No, your Grace, although I believe there was some altercation with a fire. The housekeeper was obliged to provide some ointment, your Grace, for her ladyship's hands."

"Ha! I bet that pleased the old crow, being dragged out of bed at this time of night!"

"Yes, your Grace. Well, it seems the culprit was one Mr. George Waterhouse, the same gentleman who visited last evening and remained so short a time."

"They all remained a short time, John, damn them. Go on."

"Yes, your Grace. It seemed the unfortunate gentleman met with an accident, in the shape of his lordship's sword, your Grace, wielded, I hasten to add, by his lordship's coachman."

"Dead, is he? Well, that's for the best. What of the coachman?"

"It seems Mr. Seel — I have put him in one of the *upper* rooms, your Grace — is hopeful of a happy outcome."

The Duke snorted. "Well, John. So it's all settled, is it? I suppose I can go to bed, now it's nearly dawn. See to it that that plaguey Edward don't come near me. I've no mind to have him preaching at me after all this. Sorry to have kept you up, John. You must snatch a few hours yourself. Those young 'uns are bound to sleep late."

"Yes, your Grace. Thank you, your Grace."

"Damn your eyes, John. Get me to me bed."

A few minutes later his Grace was lying comfortably in the large oaken bed he had himself chosen in the days of his youth. As the servant carefully folded the Duke's velvet coat the old man opened his eyes suddenly and fixed his man with an eagle stare. "How's the leg, John? Any improvement?"

The servant turned his wooden expression on his employer. "Thank you, your Grace, for inquiring. I am pleased to say that of late I have noticed a very marked improvement. In fact, your Grace, the limp is almost vanished."

"Is it, indeed! You're an impudent dog, John! Well, have some rest, and then set things in motion. We're going home."

WITH SOMEBODY ELSE
Theresa Charles

Rosamond sets off for Cornwall with Hugo to meet his family, blissfully unaware of the shocks in store for her.

A SUMMER FOR STRANGERS
Claire Hamilton

Because she had lost her job, her flat and she had no money, Tabitha agreed to pose as Adam's future wife although she believed the scheme to be deceitful and cruel.

VILLA OF SINGING WATER
Angela Petron

The disquieting incidents that occurred at the Vatican and the Colosseum did not trouble Jan at first, but then they became increasingly unpleasant and alarming.

DOCTOR NAPIER'S NURSE
Pauline Ash

When cousins Midge and Derry are entered as probationer nurses on the same day but at different hospitals they agree to exchange identities.

A GIRL LIKE JULIE
Louise Ellis

Caroline absolutely adored Hugh Barrington, but then Julie Crane came into their lives. Julie was the kind of girl who attracts men without even trying.

COUNTRY DOCTOR
Paula Lindsay

When Evan Richmond bought a practice in a remote country village he did not realise that a casual encounter would lead to the loss of his heart.

ENCORE
Helga Moray

Craig and Janet realise that their true happiness lies with each other, but it is only under traumatic circumstances that they can be reunited.

NICOLETTE
Ivy Preston

When Grant Alston came back into her life, Nicolette was faced with a dilemma. Should she follow the path of duty or the path of love?

THE GOLDEN PUMA
Margaret Way

Catherine's time was spent looking after her father's Queensland farm. But what life was there without David, who wasn't interested in her?

HOSPITAL BY THE LAKE
Anne Durham

Nurse Marguerite Ingleby was always ready to become personally involved with her patients, to the despair of Brian Field, the Senior Surgical Registrar, who loved her.

VALLEY OF CONFLICT
David Farrell

Isolated in a hostel in the French Alps, Ann Russell sees her fiancé being seduced by a young girl. Then comes the avalanche that imperils their lives.

NURSE'S CHOICE
Peggy Gaddis

A proposal of marriage from the incredibly handsome and wealthy Reagan was enough to upset any girl — and Brooke Martin was no exception.

A DANGEROUS MAN
Anne Goring

Photographer Polly Burton was on safari in Mombasa when she met enigmatic Leon Hammond. But unpredictability was the name of the game where Leon was concerned.

PRECIOUS INHERITANCE
Joan Moules

Karen's new life working for an authoress took her from Sussex to a foreign airstrip and a kidnapping; to a real life adventure as gripping as any in the books she typed.

VISION OF LOVE
Grace Richmond

When Kathy takes over the rundown country kennels she finds Alec Stinton, a local vet, very helpful. But their friendship arouses bitter jealousy and a tragedy seems inevitable.

CRUSADING NURSE
Jane Converse

It was handsome Dr. Corbett who opened Nurse Susan Leighton's eyes and who set her off on a lonely crusade against some powerful enemies and a shattering struggle against the man she loved.

WILD ENCHANTMENT
Christina Green

Rowan's agreeable new boss had a dream of creating a famous perfume using her precious Silverstar, but Rowan's plans were very different.

DESERT ROMANCE
Irene Ord

Sally agrees to take her sister Pam's place as La Chartreuse the dancer, but she finds out there is more to it than dyeing her hair red and looking like her sister.

HEART OF ICE
Marie Sidney

How was January to know that not only would the warmth of the Swiss people thaw out her frozen heart, but that she too would play her part in helping someone to live again?

LUCKY IN LOVE
Margaret Wood

Companion-secretary to wealthy gambler Laura Duxford, who lived in Monaco, seemed to Melanie a fabulous job. Especially as Melanie had already lost her heart to Laura's son, Julian.

NURSE TO PRINCESS JASMINE
Lilian Woodward

Nick's surgeon brother, Tom, performs an operation on an Arabian princess, and she invites Tom, Nick and his fiancé to Omander, where a web of deceit and intrigue closes about them.

THE WAYWARD HEART
Eileen Barry

Disaster-prone Katherine's nickname was "Kate Calamity", but her boss went too far with an outrageous proposal, which because of her latest disaster, she could not refuse.

FOUR WEEKS IN WINTER
Jane Donnelly

Tessa wasn't looking forward to meeting Paul Mellor again — she had made a fool of herself over him once before. But was Orme Jared's solution to her problem likely to be the right one?

SURGERY BY THE SEA
Sheila Douglas

Medical student Meg hadn't really wanted to go and work with a G.P. on the Welsh coast although the job had its compensations. But Owen Roberts was certainly not one of them!

HEAVEN IS HIGH
Anne Hampson

The new heir to the Manor of Marbeck had been found. But it was rather unfortunate that when he arrived unexpectedly he found an uninvited guest, complete with stetson and high boots.

LOVE WILL COME
Sarah Devon

June Baker's boss was not really her idea of her ideal man, but when she went from third typist to boss's secretary overnight she began to change her mind.

ESCAPE TO ROMANCE
Kay Winchester

Oliver and Jean first met on Swale Island. They were both trying to begin their lives afresh, but neither had bargained for complications from the past.